Susan K Phillips

The Last Poems of Susan K. Phillips

Susan K Phillips

The Last Poems of Susan K. Phillips

ISBN/EAN: 9783744765107

Printed in Europe, USA, Canada, Australia, Japan

Cover: Foto ©Andreas Hilbeck / pixelio.de

More available books at **www.hansebooks.com**

THE LAST POEMS OF
SUSAN K. PHILLIPS

THE LAST POEMS

OF

SUSAN K. PHILLIPS

AUTHOR OF 'ON THE SEABOARD'

'TOLD IN A COBBLE'

ETC.

LONDON

GRANT RICHARDS

9 HENRIETTA STREET

1898

Edinburgh : T. and A. CONSTABLE, Printers to Her Majesty

CONTENTS

V

CONTENTS

CONTENTS

CONTENTS

NIGHTINGALES AT GRANADA

Do you forget the starry light,
The glory of the southern night;
The wooing of the scented breeze,
That rustled all the shadowy trees;
The tinkling of the falling streams,
That mingled with our waking dreams;
And, echoing from the wooded vales,
The nightingales, the nightingales?

Do you forget how passing fair
The Moorish palace nestled there,
With arch and roof and coign and niche,
In carven beauty rare and rich;
With court and hall and corridor,
Where we two lingered, o'er and o'er,
While blent with old romantic tales
The music of the nightingales?

Do you forget the glowing noon
When, by the fountain's rhythmic tune,
We talked of all that once had been,
And peopled the calm, lonely scene
With stately forms of elder times,
Of history's lore and poet's rhymes,
And feats o'er which our fancy pales;
And thrilled through all, the nightingales?

A   I

NIGHTINGALES AT GRANADA

Do you forget those evening hours
Laden with breaths of orange-flowers,
When we, from ruddy ramparts gazing,
Saw the snow-peaks in sunset blazing;
While Darro sang his ceaseless song,
Sweeping his aloe banks along;
And, leaning on the gallery rails,
We listened to the nightingales?

And in the flush of dying day,
Down, far below, Granada lay;
While chiming from her hundred towers,
Her bells pealed out the vesper hours;
And in the soft, warm-scented hush,
The Vega smiled through roseate blush,
And, ringing through her flowery dales,
Rose up the song of nightingales.

Do you forget?   The awakening year
Is grey and cold and dreary here;
Needs but to close our tirèd eyes
And see the fairy pageant rise
Of fairy halls and rose-crowned hills,
And sweeping elms and dancing rills;
And, ere the sunny vision pales,
Once more to hear the nightingales.

UNDERSTOOD

So courtly, my darling,
  The kiss on the hand!
And I smiled as you gave it,
  For—I understand.

The words were so graceful,
  The smile was so bland;
See, I meet your eyes brightly,
  For—I understand.

Too long have we mimicked
  The old happy band,
Whose strength lies in fragments,
  Since—we understand.

What warmth is in ashes
  By memory fanned?
The flame is quite out, dear,
  And—I understand.

So I give the calm fingers,
  Stoop, kiss the cold hand,
If the pulse leaps, who knows it?
  For—I understand.

3

GONE

NEVER to see the light of love
In the keen brown eyes again,—
The eyes that brightened for my joy
And saddened for my pain.

Never to hear the cheery laugh
Or the tender, time-worn jest ;
Never to feel the hearty clasp
Of the hand he loved the best !

O brave old heart so sudden hushed,
O noble, selfless life,
O steadfast spirit, scarcely dimmed
By fourscore years of strife !

Not because Heaven is soon for thee
I weep so sore to-day,
But for the friend of half my life,
Snatched from that life away ;

For love—blind, proud, confiding love,
Such as I shall not win
Through all the time God yet may grant
My steps to wander in.

4

GONE

The sense of loss is in my heart,
A loss that knows to blend
Past, present, future, in the cry,
'Gone, O my dear old friend!'

WHY?

To grow old, to grow old, lose the gloss from the hair,
The rose from the cheek, and the flash from the eye;
To lose all things dainty, and comely, and fair;
Hard enough! but it is not for that that we care,
My heart and I.

To grow old, to grow old, to lose courage and grace,
Lose the ring from the voice that gave weakness the lie;
To feel the soft charm leave the hand and the face,
Hard enough! but that gives not our trouble its base,
My heart and I.

To grow old, to grow old, to feel faith, love, and truth,
Glowing warm as of yore under April's blue sky,
Yet to know the light pity or mockery of youth,
Doubts all—'tis for that that we sorrow, in sooth,
My heart and I.

To grow old, to grow old, while as onward we wend,
Life's lingering joys like its pale shadows fly;
Ah, closer, clasp closer, true fingers, old Friend!
So clasping we heed not how near is the end,
My heart and I.

MEMORY

THE lords of art, before us one by one
    They rise, each royal in their separate realms ;
There smiles for Claude his calm eternal sun,
    Here Raffaelle leads us to his pure-cut gems,
There Titian glows in gorgeous hues, and here
Velasquez shows his stately cavalier.

Idle to strive to number name by name
    The monarchs of all time, and tide, and race ;
Idle to shrine in careless rhymes their fame,
    To choose 'twixt Holbein's charm or Vandyck's
        grace :
Yet life has one great artist—greater still
Than all of these, adore them as we will.

One whose bright colours never fail nor fade,
    One whose soft magic cannot pass away ;
Whose canvas nothing blurs, whose tranquil shade
    Is always calm, whose light is always gay ;
Whose picture for us each is rare and rich,
As when we shrined it in our favourite niche.

Sad eyes may dazzle o'er the wondrous limning
    That makes the storied galleries so fair ;
Sad ears may tire of the world's loud hymning
    The glory of the treasures hoarded there !
But never yet was head, or heart, or eye,
That wearied of thy portraits, Memory !

7

OUTSIDE

The children played at loving,
 The boy, with the down on his lip,
And the girl, with the rose-flush on her face,
Her cooing voice, and her virgin grace ;
And they hovered about Love's mysteries
As a bird by a fountain flits and flies,
 And dares not 'light to sip.

And two who watched the pastime,—
 The man with his toil-worn frame,
And the woman with her silvered hair,
And eyes that told a story of care—
Turned to each other, with sigh and smile,
As the thought of a dream of 'a little while'
 Across their fancy came.

In the smile a touch of pity,
 As of envy in the sigh ;
It all was so pretty, and pure, and sweet,
It all was so shallow, and light, and fleet ;
Yet a blessing-prayer for the pair was blent
With the bitter-sweet that the moment lent
 To the pang of a memory.

GOOD-BYE

AND so, good-bye.
The brief, bright summer hours are gone,
The brief, bright summer days are flown;
 The holiday we snatched from life,
 From toil and moil, from care and strife,
The golden moments by the sea,
And all they held for you and me:
 Gone—like soft winds and sunny sky!
  And so, good-bye!

The land-locked air is close and dumb,
I hear the sea-voice calling 'Come';
 The heavy boughs o'erhang the grass,
 Where neither shade nor shine can pass;
And silent as the land and lea
The tones that set life's master-key.
 Ah, happy dreams, so soon they fly!
  My love, good-bye!

For ere we two again may stand
On breezy cliff or sunny sand,
 All may be changed, or lost, or dead,
 We had our hour and it is fled:
Winter will bring his bitter frost,
And Spring renew the glories lost,
 In fresh-dyed flowers and fresh-hued sky;
  But we—good-bye!

GOOD-BYE

No other year can bring to us
The rapture swift and luminous,
   The richest, fairest, and the first
   That on the sombre noontide burst.
We two may meet in calm content,
But the full cup this summer blent
   Brims once for our humanity,—
     And so, good-bye!

AFTER THE RAIN

ALL day the wild nor'-easter had swept across the
    plain,
All day against the lattice had plashed the driving
    rain;

And every budding flower, and every blade of
    grass,
Had owned the wild March weather, and bowed to
    let it pass.

Dull morn and joyless noontide had worn themselves
    away,
The sun sank sullen to the west behind a shroud of
    gray.

Sudden the great clouds parted, like a yawning
    cavern's mouth,
Soft and tender gleamed the light, the wind blew
    from the south ;

And every drooping blossom raised her fair rain-
    washed head,
The primrose glimmered 'mid her leaves, the violet
    in her bed.

Catching the golden radiance, out blazed the
    daffodil,
And from the greening hedgerows the sparrows
    twittered shrill ;

And where a woman waited, her eyes flashed back
    the light,
And with a happy smile she said, ' My love will come
    to-night.'

BY THE FIRE

SHE sat and mused by the driftwood fire,
As the leaping flames flashed high and higher,
And the phantoms of youth, as fair and bright,
Grew for her gaze in the ruddy light;
The blossoms she gathered in life's young days
Wreathed and waved in the flickering blaze,
And she laughed through a sunny mist of tears
That rose at the dream of her April years;
And ever and aye the sudden rain
Plashed on the glittering window-pane.

Sobered and saddened the pictures that showed,
As the driftwood logs to a red core glowed,
And the fancied figures of older time
Passed with the steadied step of their prime;
The daisies and snowdrops bloomed and died,
Red roses and lilies stood side by side,
While richer and fuller and deeper grew
The lines of the pictures August drew;
And ever and aye the falling rain
Streamed thick and fast on the window-pane.

The driftwood died down into feathery ash,
Where faintly and fitfully shone the flash,
Slowly and sadly her pulses beat,
And soft was the fall as of vanishing feet;

13

And lush and green as from guarded grave
She saw the grass of the valley wave,
And like echoes in ruins seemed to sigh
The 'wet west wind' that went wandering by,
And caught the sweep of the sullen rain
And dashed it against the window-pane.

MUSIC

THE music, the music, the music of the sea.
Breathing, thrilling everywhere,
Laughing in the sunny air;
Sobbing when the rushing rain
Draws a mist across the main;
Raging when the snowy spray
Dashes through the mighty bay;
And the wild nor'-westers sweep
O'er the bosom of the deep;
Always keeping sympathy with my heart and me,
The music, the music, the music of the sea.

The music, the music, the music of the sea.
Lying 'neath the southern skies,
Glorious in a thousand dyes,
Blue and gold and emerald green,
Flashing back the rainbow's sheen;
Sending gleams of snowy white
Over bay and over bight;
Crashing in long rolling waves
Far beneath the granite caves;
Always keeping sympathy with my heart and me,
The music, the music, the music of the sea.

The music, the music, the music of the sea.
Sighing in its ceaseless song,
All the sandy dunes along;

MUSIC

Murmuring to the great white stars,
Thundering 'gainst the rocky bars ;
Swaying to the crescent moon,
Rising softly o'er La Rhune ;
Calling to the sudden blast,
' 'Tis the last day ! 'Tis the last ! '
Always keeping sympathy with my heart and me,
The music, the music, the music of the sea.

REST

Where the grasses shiver
  And the curlews call,
Quiet lies my darling
  Up above it all.

All about his slumber
  The summer breezes sweep;
Softly rises to it
  The music of the deep.

When the tempests thunder
  And the great waves toss,
Steadfast o'er my darling
  Stands the tall white cross.

Far away beyond it
  Spreads the purple down;
Far away below it
  Lies the red-roofed town.

Sounds of human trouble,
  Wail of human care,
Restless hum of human woes
  Rising thickly there.

REST

Shouts of busy voices,
  Clamour of the crowd,
Clash of merry music,
  Rush of sheet and shroud.

In a mingling tumult
  Evermore they rise,
He does not heed nor hear them—
  By the cross he lies.

From the grey old tower,
  When the church-bells chime,
Sometimes kindly strangers tread
  Through the fragrant thyme.

On the tended flowers
  They look and turn away;
'See how some one loves him yet,'
  Wondering, they say.

And when twilight closes
  Over sea and land,
'Mid those tended flowers
  Moves a quiet hand.

And the lips of her who loves him
  Press on the cold grey stone,
She says, 'Good night, my darling,'
  And passes on alone.

BELONGS

'Do you know her as belongs to him?' the grey-haired
    fisherman said,
Standing beside the tended flowers, by the Cross, on
    the rocky Head.
'I can't call her name to mind, though I knows her
    well enough;
I've seen her pass under summer suns, seen her when
    gales are rough;
She scarcelins lets a day go by but she climbs the
    steps up here:
If you look aside to the Colonel's Cross, you'll mostlins
    see her near.'

'Her as belongs to him!' And far away from the great
    white Cross,
Passing along her household ways, with the aching
    sense of loss
Weighing ever the heavier upon weary head and heart,
Because from all he left on earth, fate forced her life
    apart;
The simple phrase from the honest lips, sent by a
    loving hand,
Brought comfort, they who have loved and lost alone
    could understand.

'LORD, KEEP MY MEMORY GREEN'

'LORD, keep my memory green.' Ay, them's grand
    words!
I got our Bill to write 'em plainly down,
See thee, upon yon sheet; an' they were said
    By some great chap, up there i' Lunnon town:
I reckon as he knowed above a bit
What Natur' is, to give them words to it.

I 've had my ups and downs like other folk,
    Though now I 'se laid up safe an' snug i' port;
There 's not a warmer fireside 'long the shore,
    An' not a bonnier window in the court.
Press to the pane, bairn; now just bend thysen,
Thou 'lt get a glint o' blue waves tossing then.

Yet as I sits an' hes my pipe, an' stirs
    The driftlog on the hearth, it 's not to think
How the wind sets, nor yet to guess what Sal
    Has got for supper-time, for bit or drink;
I 'se mostlins far away, an' dreaming like
Of how the sun would rise on Rhosdale Pike;

An' the old farmhouse, nestled in its shade,
    Ablaze with golden lichens on the thatch;
An' how I used to hide among the fern
    After the milking-horn wer' blown, to catch
A word—an' mebby a kiss, too—frev her
Who gave me them two sprays o' lavender.

20

'LORD, KEEP MY MEMORY GREEN'

Poor, bonnie Annie !—She wer' over good
   For me, her father said,—a common lad
Striving to get a living down the Staithes,
   A crazy coble all the wealth I had ;
An' he'd an acre of his own, an' cows,
An' routh of plenishing about the house.

An' so they parted us ; but for all that,
   We met one July gloaming on the moor,
Behind the rowans on the cairn, an' she
   Swore she would keep her troth-plight fast and sure ;
An' sore we sobbed an' close we clung together,
We two young fools, out 'mid the budding heather.

An' I gi'ed her a bit o' crimson weed
   I'd fund among the rocks at Runswick Bay,
An' she gi'ed me them sprays o' lavender—
   The bush still grows beside the gate, I lay.
Our Bill's a handy chap ; he framed 'em—see,
An' wrote them words beneath 'em fair for me.

That very night they pressed me ; war-time then
   Kept every man safe-barred within his door,
But I wer' desperate, an' they pounced on me,
   Lounging, half-sullen, down upon the shore ;
I gi'ed in, stupid-like—I scarcelins cared,
Parted from her, or how or where I fared.

Then came a time o' work an' throng an' change,
   An' fighting fierce, out upon stranger seas ;
An' jolly nights o' singing with our mates
   Down by the galley-fire, when the breeze
Wer' lound, an' times o' storm and tempest too—
Well, there wer' much to win, as well as rue.

'LORD, KEEP MY MEMORY GREEN'

An' by an' by I got my rise, an' stood
  Bosun, no less, an' wi' my pay an' rank
Knew I might gang and ask for Annie straight—
  A sweetheart any lass might smile to thank
For heart and hearth. Well, well, for all I 'se seen,
Of those glad dreams, Lord, keep my memory green.

For all I landed just a year too late,
  An' fund her happy in another's home,
An' heard her laugh beside another's bairn,
  To bid her old companion frankly come
To taste her cheer, an' sit aside on her,
An' jest about them sprays o' lavender,

I tell thee, bairn, I mind like yesterday
  How, when I 'd joked an' drunk my mug of ale,
An' made as I 'd forgotten all we hoped,
  Boasting above a bit to tell the tale
Of all I 'd done an' won, an' left her there,
Set on a creepie by her master's chair,

I sought our tryst beneath the rowan-trees,
  An' sate me on the moor, an' like a bairn
Cried for the days when I had held her close
  In the soft gloaming by the rocky cairn.
Well, well! it 's past and gone; it 's nobbut queer
To think, what hurt one so, grows a'most dear.

I wonder if she hes my bit o' weed,
  An' if it keeps its bonnie colour yet?
Hidden, as women use such things to hide,
  To look at, when they has a mind to fret?
Mebby, for all that is an' might ha' been,
She, too, may care to keep her memory green.

'LORD, KEEP MY MEMORY GREEN'

Tho' pride an' love gi'ed me a cruel turn,
   I 'se lived to think it better as it is.
Folk say our Annie 's summat of a shrew,
   An' peace is better than a storm or kiss ;
Our Jack wer' drowned off Sheerness, an' his Bill
Keeps my bit spot frev growing over still.

'Uncle 's ' as good a sound as 'feyther '—eh?
   An' I 'se my awn way by my hearth an' all ;
An' yet I keeps my sprays o' lavender,
   An' loves to see 'em hanging on the wall.
Bitter an' blessed the times that I ha' seen,
An' so they serve to keep my memory green.

AT TOR BAY

Sunlight over the sea,
The golden sunlight of May,
Where the long blue rollers flash to white
   In beautiful Tor Bay.

Sunlight over the hills
Crowned by a hundred homes,
That smile as the rosy sunset sinks
   Over the Devon combes.

Sunlight over the woods,
Clad in their first pure green,
Where the chestnut shows his stately spikes,
   And the birches flash between.

Sunlight over the flowers—
The thousand flowers that blow
Where the ivies garb the dark red rocks,
   And the tinkling streamlets flow.

And a cloud in the dreamy eyes
That are gazing far away,
Over tossing leagues of the sea that rolls
   In beautiful Tor Bay.

DREAMING

I DREAMED as I slept last night.
    And because the wild wind blew,
And because the plash of the angry rain,
Fell heavily on the window-pane,
I heard in my dream the sob of the main,
    On the seaboard that I knew.

I dreamed as I slept last night.
    And because the oaks outside
Swayed and groaned to the rushing blast,
I heard the crash of the stricken mast,
And the wailing shriek as the gale swept past ;
    And cordage and sail replied.

I dreamed as I slept last night.
    And because my heart was there,
I saw where the stars shone large and bright,
And the heather budded upon the height,
With the Cross above it standing white ;
    My dream was very fair.

I dreamed as I slept last night.
    And because of its charm for me,
The inland voices had power to tell
Of the sights and sounds I love so well,
And they rapt my fancy in the spell
    Wove only by the sea.

SHIPWRECK WOOD

SEE how the firelight flashes on the pane !
    Look how it flickers to the raftered roof !
That almost gives its brightness back again,
    So far the darkling shadows hold aloof.
See how it dances, and the warmth is good ;
But all my fire is made of shipwreck wood.

Jem brought these furs from his first voyage back ;
    Will found these beads, one day at Elsinore ;
And the gold band that clasps my ruffles, Jack
    Bought me with half his pay, at Singapore.
Each speaks of love and strength and hardihood ;
But all my fire is made of shipwreck wood.

The sea is roaring over 'wandering graves,'
    Where all my best and bravest lie at peace;
I hear a requiem in the moaning waves,
    That only with my parting breath will cease.
The sea has given me work and warmth and food ;
But all my fire is made of shipwreck wood.

THE CURATE

WHAT did he know about it—the boy who stood up
  there,
In the quaint old oak 'three-decker' in the ancient
  house of prayer?

No sign of modern culture had touched the building
  old,
Whose strong square tower had crowned the Head for
  centuries untold.

The brown, worm-eaten benches were ranged in order
  due,
And high amid the galleries, proud reigned 'the squire's
  pew.'

And names for long forgotten spoke dumbly from the
  wall,
While through the latticed windows came the billows'
  rise and fall.

What did he know about it—the boy with earnest face,
Standing above the worshippers, in the solemn, time-
  worn place?

There were hoary heads below him, and faces lined by
  need,
They had stol'n from empty board and hearth, to ask
  the Lord to heed.

27

To the worn and weary pilgrims on life's hard down-
    ward way,
What, from his fearless starting-point, had the young
    lips to say?

What could he know about it?   Had those bright,
    eager eyes
Seen once below the surface of our mortal miseries?

The sin, the doubt, the sorrow, the emptiness of life,
The bitter, strong temptation—the failing, fainting
    strife?

The girding-on the armour to fight the battle on,
With victory's hope and guerdon alike for ever gone?

The broken dream, the shaken trust, the loss, the
    wrong, the fall,—
Ah! boyhood in its happy spring, what could it know
    of all?

The sea roared on below us, the winds above us swept,
The voice went flowing onward, the old folk stared or
    slept,

And with a rueful sigh and smile, one glanced from
    them to him,
While the sunset touched the Cross to gold, but left
    the chancel dim.

THE FISHERMAN IN THE COUNTRY

THE land-locked air is warm and sweet,
The land-locked breeze is soft to meet ;
The land-locked path lies smooth and green,
Where golden sunlights fleck between
The foliage of the elm and ash ;
And bright the land-locked waters flash
Past ferny bank and mossy grot,
All blue with the forget-me-not.

But I, amid the daisied leas,
And the cool shade of spreading trees,
While in sweet chorus finch and thrush
Make music in the scented bush,—
I want the wild wind, fresh and free,
That sweeps across the northern sea—
The keen, strong wind that blows to give
The room to breathe, the strength to live.

My foot falls soundless on the turf,
I want the thunder of the surf;
The inland tones are low and soft,
I want the voice that rings aloft,
When the fierce squall through sheet and shroud
Calls for the seaman's strength aloud,
And hand and heart are strong to brave
The terrors of the wind and wave.

THE FISHERMAN IN THE COUNTRY

We on the seaboard learn to face,
Each standing steadfast in his place,
Death, in his aspects manifold—
Of hunger, shipwreck, want, and cold;
Life, stern and earnest, learns to love
The strife below, the storm above.
Fair is your world of flowers and trees—
I hear the calling of the seas.

THE CROSS

Where the wild white breakers surge and play,
On the blue of beautiful Biarritz Bay;
Where the mighty clouds of snowy spray
Toss to the skies of the southern day,
On the jagged rock, a bow-shot from land,
The sacred symbol is raised to stand,
With its dumb, sad record of storm and loss,—
For men know, as they look at the low white cross,
That there, close to safety and love and home,
Strong lives were spent in the hell of foam
That swept all help aside.

Lingering out on the ' Virgin's Rock,'
Hearing the ceaseless thundering shock,
Seeing the rollers meet and lock,
One feels how the sea at the men may mock !
Skill, and science, and strength may meet,
But the might of the waves is hard to beat;
By the bit of timber left swaying yet,
Over the restless heave and fret,
We know where, beneath the furious gale,
Shivered were bulwarks and rent the sail
As the deadly strife was tried.

And the nameless mariners lost that night,
When Biarritz watched 'neath the pert stars' light,

31

And her fishermen strove, with baffled might,
To snatch their prey from the waves' wild white ;
Quiet they lie where the little cross
Stands steadfast above the crash and toss,
Where wondering strangers come to gaze,
And the long waves break through the sunny days ;
Where the stern cliffs over their tumult frown,
And the Virgin looks serenely down
Through the ebb and flow of tide.

RUDDERLESS

WELL for the boat, when the pilot
 Stands steady, his hand on the helm ;
Well, for no cross-current takes it,
 No swift, sudden squall can o'erwhelm

True as the compass she carries,
 With her sail set, whatever the blast,
As the light of the long day slopes westward,
 She glides to her haven at last.

But the bark tossed from flowing to ebbing,
 While the wild wind is shifting about,
Dazed by the glitter of pleasure,
 Swept by the tempest of doubt ;

Caught in the cruel back-water,
 Wooed by the treacherous gleam,
Till shore, sky, and ocean together,
 Show vague as the things of a dream ;

Ill for such vessel,—yet heaven
 Built her, fitted her, sent her afloat ;
God's harbours are many and open,
 He may pilot the rudderless boat.

BABY

ANOTHER day of life and laughter
   Its course has run;
Another night comes stealing after,
   Son of my son.
Little feet are tired of running,
   Little fingers of their quest,
Little head with curls o'er-running,
   Droops for its rest.

When the rosy dawning hours
   Say night is done,
Wake with birds, and bees, and flowers,
   Son of my son.
Wake the happy laughter trilling
   From the sweet lips dewy red;
Merry baby fancies filling
   Dainty gold head.

Stretch the fair round arms in meeting,
   Love lightly won,
Crow and coo your pretty greeting,
   Son of my son.
Oh, the soft curls tossed and tumbling,
   Eyes like violets dark with dew;
Eager feet that strive in stumbling,
   Keen will to do!

BABY

Every moment brings a pleasure,
   Seized and done,
Every toy a transient treasure,
   Son of my son.
Time, a fearless, fresh possessing,
   Life, a thing all mirth and joy ;
Fenced by love and crowned with blessing,
   God keep our boy !

RHYME

PLAYING with words—the pretty toys!—
Whose charm nor time nor tide destroys.
Age, subtly creeping, steals away
The step's light spring, the glances gay,
The joyous echo from the tone,
The laugh that youth can match alone;
But this defies the touch of time,
The gladness of the ringing rhyme.

The mellow metre sounds as clear
As ever to the April ear;
The trumpet-call of martial song
Can bid the sober pulses throng
As gallantly as when, of old,
They thrilled to hear the summons told;
And tired fingers yet can chime
A melody for ringing rhyme.

I send a gay defiance back,
As, treading on my downward track,
'Mid moaning winds and fading flowers,
And thickening graves, and darkened hours,
I wake the sweet old magic still,
I feel my hand obey my will;
Take up the glove that's flung by Time,
And challenge him in ringing rhyme.

MAY MORN AT GIBRALTAR

THE sweet May morn in English lanes :
Through lush green grasses creak the wains,
The violets from their mosses peep,
The primroses in sunshine sleep,
Fresh from the wash of April rains.

Here, where the tideless sea complains,
The sun its blaze of noontide gains,
O'er mountain shadows, purple deep,
This sweet May morn.

Over the Rock the west winds sweep,
Harvest of perfumed airs to reap ;
Yet dazzled northern eyesight strains
For pale blue skies and daisied plains,
Where dewy England laughs to keep
This sweet May morn.

ON THE ROCK

HERE the snowdrifts shudder
To the north wind's shock :
Do the sunbeams glance and play
Out on the Rock?
Here the bitter frost is lord
Over glen and lea. :
Do your south winds whisper to
The tideless sea?

Here the hoar-fringed ivies droop
From the cottage eaves :
Do the dewdrops diamond all
Your roses' leaves?
Here we gather round the hearth,
Stir the leaping flames :
Do you trace the haunts that bear
Old storied names?

Here we watched with yearning thoughts,
Through long nights and days,
As the great ship thundered on
Vague ocean ways ;
Did you, as the white stars throbbed,
Hot suns rose and set,
Think of those you left behind,
Those, wistful yet?

ON THE ROCK

Here the void is aching,
For we weep to miss
All the strong protective love,
Hand, and eye, and kiss.
Is love so strong, that absence
It can soothe or mock:
Do you keep our places still,
Out on the Rock?

WATCHING

Watching, where the sunset dies
In the grey of rain-charged skies,
   Wearily, so wearily;
While the low winds sweeping past
Shake the leaves that lingering last,
   Clothe the branches drearily.

Watching, where the garden shows
Sodden grass and drooping rose,
   Last of all its greenery;
While the chill mist, like a veil,
Spreads its empire, cold and pale,
   O'er the distant scenery.

Turning where the ruddy blaze
Round the high-piled oak-logs plays,
   Through the dim hall glimmering;
The fair girl by the hearthstone stood,
The spirit of its solitude,
   The red light round her shimmering.

Pushing back her falling hair,
With parted lips and eager air,
   Rapt in trance of listening,
While in her eyes, so soft and blue,
The slowly gathering drops of dew
   Were in the firelight glistening.

WATCHING

The silence round her grew intense,
The falling ash had eloquence,
   The sobbing wind wailed meaningly;
And to the half-unconscious gaze,
One form seemed fashioned in the blaze,
   As if it neared her, dreamingly.

The dog crept slowly to her knee,
And looked up at her wistfully;
   The charring logs burnt cheerily;
But lower drooped the golden head;
'He will not come to me,' she said,
   Wearily, so wearily.

HE AND SHE

SHE—where the deer were couching,
  In the broad oak's shadow dark,
And the merry beck was dancing down
  The green glades of the park;
Where the skylark's song was trilling,
  Away in the world of blue,
And the busy bees were seeking
  The hill where the heather grew.

He—on the deck of the steamer,
  As its ocean way it ploughed,
While the wild west wind was making
  Music in sheet and shroud;
Where the seagulls screamed and swooped above
  The long white track of foam,
And over the great Atlantic
  The 'clipper' thundered home.

From the heart of each was rising,
  From the green glade and the sea,
'God bless and keep my darling,
  For love, and life, and me!'
And the angel who guards true lovers,
  As he hovered the twain above,
Bore the prayers, blent both together,
  To the feet of the God of Love.

'BE OF GOOD CHEER'

I HAVE my cruse of oil,
I have my cake of meal ;
I am worn with life's long toil,
The threads are few on the reel.
One by one from the ranks fall out
The mates who joined them with cheer and shout,
When the merry march in the morn begun,
Under the laugh of the rising sun ;
One by one they drop to the grave,
Where the pale stars gleam and the grasses wave ;
On the surcoat is rent and soil,
The dents are deep on the steel,
Yet I have my cruse of oil,
I have my cake of meal.

Low sinks the cruse of oil,
Spare grows the cake of meal,
Yet the lees no bitters spoil,
No thieves my grain can steal ;
And though my step be faint and slow,
Still cheerily on my path I go,
And prize the joy that is left to me,
In the rush of wind and the roar of sea.

43

And welcome the blossoms blooming still,
Where the valley lies at foot of the hill;
For, tangled although the coil
I gather from Fortune's wheel,
It is Memory pours my oil,
It is Love who grinds my meal.

NOT ALONE

Is it not very lonely,
   As you sit by the lighted hearth,
Whence change and death have banished
   The voices of youth and mirth?

Is it not very lonely,
   When the winter firelight plays
On the empty chairs in the silent room,
   So full in the bygone days?

Is it not very lonely,
   When the summer gloaming falls,
And the only eyes that answer yours
   Gleam out from the darkening walls?

'No, I am never lonely,'
   The quiet woman said;
'I people the world I live in,
   With the figures of my dead.

'They look on me from their pictures,
   They speak in the sound of seas,
In the bird that chirps at the window,
   In the whispering of the trees.

45

NOT ALONE

'They sit in the chair beside me,
  With the books that they made my own;
And so I am never lonely,
  Although so much alone.'

EXPERIENCE

AND still, and pale, and cold Experience sat;
She heard where Hope awoke his golden measure;
She saw where Love gave Life his wealth to treasure.
While with triumphant smile defying Fate,
To spoil what he, he only, could create,
He built, in a sweet hour of laughing leisure,
A palace, fit for Passion and for Pleasure,
To furl their glittering wings and dwell thereat.
And still Experience waited; on each hand,
With subtle mockery kindling in their eyes,
Time and Satiety took up their stand,
And watched with her the fairy fabric rise;
Then, with her long, lean hand she touched the wall,
And lo! it fell, and utter was its fall.

THE CHRISTMAS ROSE

'Why must I only bloom 'mid frost and snows,
Under these grey skies?' said the Christmas rose;
'Why must I know no joy of April showers,
Smile to no sunshine, hail no golden hours
Of warmth and loveliness?   As pure my leaves
As the white lily, queen of summer eves;
As fair my foliage clusters for the breeze
As the sweet violets 'neath the willow-trees.
I claim my right, the seasons I defy,
And ope my petals to the August sky.'

The red rose saw, and blushed in angry pride;
The lily saw, and shivered from her side;
The gorgeous darlings of the trim parterre
Gazed on the pale intruder standing there,
And with the scornful wonder in their eyes,
Scorched her, as scorched the bright indignant skies
That shone down on her, in a withering glow;
And the light wind laughed, mockingly and low;
To the hard earth she bowed her humbled head,
'Time and the world are very hard,' she said.

LIFE'S AUTUMN

THE snowdrop and the violet are dead,
　　The rich red rose has shed her petals rare ;
Look, where the lily raised her queenly head,
　　But withered stalk and crumbling leaves are there ;
And soft and sad the wind of autumn sighs
Over dank uplands, under low grey skies.

Yet every wood-walk gleams beneath the rays
　　Of the pale sunlight, in a splendour dressed
Of gold and crimson, such as April days
　　Can scarcely show, when pranked in all her best
The dying leaves, like the sun's afterglow,
In death the fulness of their glory show.

Take home the lesson, Life, in flush of youth,
　　And golden noontide of maturity ;
Gather the precious flowers of love and truth,
　　Of patience, kindliness, and sympathy.
The unfading leaves of every angel bloom
Will light and smooth the pathway to the tomb.

THE OLD ROOM

THE room the same; the same old curtains draped
  About the deep bay window ; by the hearth
The same old chair, deep carven, quaintly shaped,
  That served us once as theme for careless mirth;
Tears gather through the smile I force to-night,
To see it in the leaping firelight.

There is the sofa, where I stooped to smooth
  The thick curls from his forehead,—on yon shelf
We kept our books, the treasures of our youth,
  The shrines of hope and dream, and second self:
How thick the dust upon their pages lies—
The lore that does not suit to modern eyes!

And he is sleeping where the tall white cross
  Watches the long heave of the Northern Sea ;
And I, with the deep marks of wrong and loss,
  Deeper than time had traced them, changing me,
Stand, all alone, 'mid the dumb witness borne
Of the old room, the same in life's sweet morn.

APART

I close my eyes, because the mocking light
   Will shine upon your empty chair, my own;
   I shut my ears, because the low wind's tone
Will mimic my sad wail for you to-night.

I clasp my fingers in a passionate prayer
   That God will guard you, guide you, watch, and
      bless;
   For they will tremble for the soft caress
That but an hour ago you planted there.

I take the volume that we love, my heart,
   Striving to force my fancy 'neath its spell.
   In vain, in vain!   Life throbs, 'Farewell, farewell.'
We love, we trust; but oh, we are apart!

REMEMBRANCE

Do you forget it, love, the sweet old phrase?
  Do you forget the clasp of hand in hand,
  The gesture we two only understand?
The magic lying in the dear old ways?
The glow of passion in its morning days
  Has softened to the evening, where we stand
  Watching the wavelets break upon the sand,
In the soft reflex of the sunset rays.
Dear, the sweet roses that we gathered then
  Are faded quite, and the pale twilight sees
Night-blowing lilies glimmer, each a gem,
  Beneath the low boughs of the yellowing trees;
But oh! their scent is rich and subtle yet;
I prize the fragrance, dear.   Do you forget?

TOLERANCE

THE question held its empire of an hour,
The hearts of men grew heavy, stern, and hot ;
Till Courtesy shrank back, and calm forgot
Its lulling spell ; and Truth's seraphic power
Paled, as at lightning flash a fragile flower ;
Till even Love shared in the common lot
Amid the babel, that remembered not
The grace and sweetness that was once its dower.
And solemn names were tossed like idle toys
Into the whirlwind of unlovely doom ;
Sudden—a hush fell on the angry noise,
As passed amid the stifling, lurid gloom
An angel, with grave smile and pitying glance ;
And men, repentant, called her—Tolerance.

HUSH!

'HUSH!' said the brook, down dancing from the moor,
'He cometh, brushing through the purple bloom';
'Hush!' said the water-lily : 'he will come
And choose, amid my blossoms white and pure,
A love-gift.' 'Hush!' the low wind laughed ; 'for sure
As the lark wavers earthward to her home,
He seeks the tryst where Love completes the sum,
That gives to life the joy that can endure.'
And the girl, blushing, heard the happy speech
That murmured round her, while white fingers played
Amid the ripples, 'neath the willow's shade,
And learnt the lore that Nature mocked to teach.
But over flower and stream the twilight crept,
And the lone watcher bowed her head and wept.

AT BRIMHAM CRAGS

Down from the moorland swept the August breeze,
Across the wilderness of rock and heather,
Bowing rich bloom and clustering fern together,
While from the gleam of crimson bilberries
Boomed the low humming of the busy bees ;
And the eternal Crags, that stand for ever,
From April's laugh to frown of wintry weather,
Tossed to its call that crown of rowan-trees.
The glorious sun sloped slowly to the west,
That blushed a roseate welcome to her lord ;
And springing sudden from her lowly nest,
To the rich air the lark her triumph poured ;
And as the carol thrilled and rang o'erhead,
'God keep my darling safe for me,' she said.

AT BAYONNE

WHERE the twin spires gleam against the sky,
Where southern sunshine dazzles from the blue,
Where the great rivers meet in rolling through
The old historic city,—days gone by
Unfold themselves for English heart and eye,
Recalling all our fathers dared to do ;
When the proud eagles, beaten backwards, flew,
And here, at Bayonne, lit, to live or die.
Ah, still St. Etienne, where the peasants meet,
And laugh and chatter through the holiday,—
How the fierce battle hurtled through thy street,
Where, round thy altar, England stood at bay !
Peace broods above the two fair realms at last,
And here we dream of all the furious past.

ALL SAINTS' DAY

THROUGH storied panes the winter sunshine crept,
The thunder music rolled along the nave,
And, far and faint, the answer of the wave,
As the low wind around the grey tower swept,
With the long notes recurrent measure kept;
And some, thanksgiving for their darlings gave,
And some, fresh mourners from the new-made grave,
Bowed stricken heads upon their hands, and wept.
The preacher's voice arose, serene and calm,
Telling of saints' pure joys in Paradise;
And, rising ever with the chant and psalm
To the eternal temple of the skies,
'Trust Him who died to save,' the sea voice said;
'Trust Him with all—the living and the dead.'

THE HALL

THE dear old house, steadfast and calm it stands,
  Four-square and strong to all the winds that blow ;
The stately centre of the subject-lands,
  Just as men built it, centuries ago.
The water-lilies waver on the lake,
  The pigeons wheel and circle round the cote,
And from the shade the great yew-hedges make,
  Swells the soft music of the thrush's note ;
And fair in sweeping change of light and dark,
  The woods crown all the summits of the hills,
Where rich in hollowed uplands lies the park,
  Where, glittering plainward, dance a hundred rills ;
And looking on the home I love, I say,
God bless its owners ever, as to-day !

IN OCTOBER

THE chill October rain is falling,
Wearily falling the whole day long;
Like the sound of an ancient tale of wrong,
The wild west wind through the woods is calling;
Like a spell the fair sad earth enthralling,
The wailing forms to a funeral song.
The chill October rain is falling,
Wearily falling the whole day long,
Its notes the lingering flowers appalling;
The last red rose-leaves drifting throng
From the ivy clusters green and strong,
The breath of our sweet lost June recalling:
While the chill October rain is falling.

THE PLEA

'It was so sweet and lovely in its youth.'
So Memory pleaded, while her tender hand
Strove round the drooping leaves to draw a band,
As helpful as the broken strands of truth.
'The past's lost glory dims the present more,'
He answered, with his clear eyes bright with scorn.
'Yet,' whispered Memory, 'when it first was born,
So many weakling leaves you saw, and bore.'
'Ay, for I thought that ever at its root
Were Love and Faith,' replied the sweet, proud voice.
'And can no penitence, no second choice,
No pledge renewed, restore its blighted life?'
'My utter trust met treachery,' he said;
And Memory heard, and left the pale bloom dead.

ASLEEP

Hope in the heart his watch is keeping,
Waiting, waiting, till love shall wake;
Waiting the happy hush to break,
Joy to his side is softly creeping.
Who dare rouse him from his sleeping?
Time may be bringing pang and ache;
Waiting, waiting till love shall wake.
Hope in the heart his watch is keeping,
Fancy a thousand flowers is heaping,
Faith shows her golden corn for reaping;
But ah! who dares the glass to take,
Or the precious golden sand to shake?
Hope in the heart his watch is keeping,
But the love that sleeps may but wake for weeping.

TRIUMPHANT

UNDER the chestnut-tree the weeds they burned;
Their fragrance floated on the brooding air,
That scarcely stirred the branches growing bare,
As for the dying autumn's smile they yearned.
The smoke rose slowly upward, and unrolled
Its lazy, lingering banner 'neath the sky;
And through the pale blue haze shone gorgeously
The chestnuts' broadening fans of living gold.
The low wind freshened, blowing from the north,
And swept the smoke-mist from the scene away,
And in the splendour of the closing day
The great leaves flashed unclouded glory forth.
So feeble speech a noble faith obscures,
But the words perish, and the creed endures.

HIS PLACE

To the soft stillness of the shadowed room,
Where the red embers crumble in their heat,
And the low gleam falls on your favourite seat,
And rosy lamp-light makes a pleasant gloom,
With tirèd step and tirèd thought I come.
I want the flashing of your smile to meet,
I want the clasping of your hand to greet,
I want your presence, the deep heart of home.
Dear, in the battle of the busy life,
Where the great pulse of England's being chimes
Amid the lulls and rallies of the strife,
Does the faint whisper of the sweet old times
Creep through the turmoil, breathing, ' Fall or win,
Your place is kept, none else may venture in '?

TANGLE-TOPS

Ay ! we 've queer names among us.—There 's Scaddie,
    an' Cud, an' Flick,
An' yon big chap, laughing yonder, they calls him Sugar
    Dick.

Nay, I forgets their crisun-names—they scarcelins know
    theirsels,
Afloat or ashore alike, you see, they never gets aught
    else.

An' if a chap once gets a name, it 's rare it iver drops,
I 'll tell thee how one cam' to be—him we calls Tangle-
    tops.

T' rock 's none safe for strangers, till t' tide has ebbed
    a bit ;
Come, yon auld boat 's a shelter, we 'll talk when pipes
    are lit.

What ! summat 's moving on t' Scar ?   It 's him we 're
    talking on ;
He 's safe enow: he 's allis there, an' knows it stone
    by stone,

An' reads 'em as thou might'st a book, an' spells both
    wind an' wave—
I reckon t' great grey sea to him is like a crowded
    grave.

Poor chap! I lay he's reason. He's wrinkled now an'
    brown,
Just like t' strands o' tangle t' bairns drag up t' town.

An' nobbut fourteen year ago, he wer' a stalwart lad,
Wi' bright keen eyes, an' springing foot, an' a laugh
    that made one glad.

Poor Jack!—he 'd got no by-name then—he came down
    here wi' Nance,
She saw t' sunshine strike t' Nab, and t' wild white
    horses prance,

An' she wer' for a sail, thou seest, i' t' boat he 'd scratted
    to get:
She lay by t' Staithes all taut an' trim, her paint wer'
    a'most wet.

We told her as t' wind wer' shy, an' t' clouds wer'
    driving fast:
She just looked up at him an' laughed, an' got her way
    at last.

He hove t' sail, she took t' helm: we shouted from
    t' pier,
But they shot her ower t' harbour bar, wi' neither wit
    nor fear.

E   65

An' by they'd gone an hour or so, t' clouds packed
    black i' t' west,
T' wind swept down, t' breakers rose, an' thou canst
    guess t' rest.

Needed a stronger hand than hers to keep t' helum
    straight,
When t' sheet wer' gyving in t' storm—he hadn't ta'en
    his mate.

There's none as knows t' right on it, but when t' squall
    was spent,
Along t' beach and ower t' Scar, fearful an' sad we went ;

An' just below t' Black Nab's reef we fund t' shattered
    boat,
An' tossing out on t' angry sea, wer' summat pink
    afloat.

She'd a kerchief round her bonnie neck—a pink 'un,
    t' lasses said ;
An' 'mid t' brash at Saltwick lay Jack—we thought him
    dead.

We'd wark to loosen frev his arm a mass o' weed he'd
    got ;—
T' Scar's nigh clear, we'll gang just now, I'll take thee
    tu t' spot.

I lay he thought 'twas Nance he held, for when he opes
    his eyes,
'Keep still, my lass—I'll save thee yet!' wer' t' first
    words he cries.

Poor chap! he just went dateless, and frev that day to
    this,
In shine or shade, in foul or fair, thou 'lt never find him
    miss

His weary ram'lins to an' fro, about an' round t' rock;
He'll get a crab or fossil whiles, but he 's main dazed wi'
    t' shock.

He doan't know what he 's seeking, but when t' squall
    sweeps down,
An' t' breakers rise an' t' fret comes up, and hides t'
    red-roofed town,

He 'll moan an' grope where t' tangle grows thick as a
    woodland copse,
An' nurse it like a bairn, an' so they calls him Tangle-
    tops.

He 's but a-dowly puttin' on, he fends as best he can—
It 's no use heaving watter over a drownded man.

There 's many a bitter story told between t' wind an'
    t' sea,
Although there 's not a spot on earth like Whitby Bay
    to me.

Give him a bit o' baccy, that cheers him up a bit,
But as for argeying with him—no sort o' use in it.

An' if a stranger hails him, like one half-dazed he stops;
If they ask him what they calls him, he 'll tell 'em,
    Tangle-tops.

AT ST. SEBASTIAN

Far, and near, and wide they sleep,
   Who die for England's sake ;
Where never love can its vigil keep,
   Where never the hearts that ache
Can come to tend the happy flowers
   That spring, as to mock our tears,
In the bloom that returns with summer hours,
   Through all the varying years.

Very far and wide they sleep
   Who die for England's sake ;
Yet never, I think, could the charnel gloom
   So fair an aspect take,
As where the southern sunshine lights
   The long Biscayan waves,
And the fort on St. Sebastian's heights
   Stands over the English graves.

O'er their graves who died in the fierce assault,
   Those guarded walls to win ;
Do the restless rollers remember yet
   How their eternal din
Was lost in the cheer and the battle-cry,
   Borne on the startled blast,
As St. George's banner, borne on high,
   Crowned the great fort at last ?

AT ST. SEBASTIAN

Very quietly do they lie,
    Our heroes, laid asleep,
Where round St. Clara's fairy isle
    The breakers surge and sweep ;
Where the gorse and the broom flash living gold
    To the blaze of the noonday sun,
And high above stands the mighty hold,
    By English valour won.

The old familiar names stand out
    To the wistful English eyes :
The old familiar tales of fame
    Wake 'neath the stranger skies ;
The foreign tones and accents sound
    Like voices in a dream,
So homelike do the names around
    To the English wanderers seem.

Very quietly they lie,
    Till the last parade shall come,
And the long roll of England's dead
    Hear Heaven's own muster-drum.
Ah, stately height 'neath the Spanish sky,
    Take the trust our fathers gave,
When, after their dear-bought victory,
    They left 'neath your turf the brave.

THE LAST WHALER

An' so they can't spare space for her to rot!—
I'd had a thow't they would ha' let her be,
For sake of the old days they've all forgot,
An' we might pass together, her an' me—
    Me, to my sleep up 'mid them crowding graves,
    An' her, to better rest, aneath the waves.

But there,—the river's nigh ckoked up wi' all
Them ugly steamboats, as ha' made sike deed,
Wi' their red sides, like a great iron wall,
An' their black funnels, promising o' speed;
    There's many a chap has put his hard-earned brass
    I' them, and hungered for his pains, alas !

An' times are hard; and they will do to sell
The timbers that ha' braved the Arctic seas,
When she went dancing o'er the ocean swell
Wi' all her canvas given to the breeze;
    There's none so many left frev these old days,
    To tell her story while she feeds the blaze.

I wer' a proud chap when, as specksioneer,
I trod her deck, the gallant *Northern Star*,
As she went gliding past the crowded pier,
An' clove the breakers surging on the bar ;
    I mind how Nancy looked, so fresh and fair,
    Wi' my blue ribbon in her golden hair.

Waving her little hand while tears ran over,
　Yet couldn't wash the dimpling smile away;
You see, she didn't care to send her lover
Without a cheer upon the parting day;
　An' we had pledged our words as we'd be wed,
　The Sabbath after she should make the Head.

When we came home—our banns were out, you see,
　But her auld mother wouldn't ha' her left
Neither a wife nor widow like—an' she,
Knowing t'auld dame wer' half o' sense bereft
　Sin' her poor man wer' drownded—made her give
　Consent—'she'd none so much time left to live.'

'None so much time'—we thow't so! I won home,
　Both proud an' happy. Many a full-fed fish
Had fallen to my harpoon, an' I'd the sum
O' gain and glory given to my wish.
　Who met us on the pier as we cam' back?—
　Why, her auld mother, clad i' rusty black!

My Nancy loved the bonnie primrose flowers,
　My mate had sought the roots an' set 'em thick
About her grave, hard by the Abbey Towers:
An' when I could—I lay a gey bit sick—
　I climbed the steps, an' knelt them blooms beside,
　An' when the soft leaves touched me, why, I cried—

Cried like a bairn; they say it saved my wits:
　It may ha' been so—like a bitter dream
Of wrong, an' loss, an' hope, that came by fits,
As 'gainst a thunder-crash the lightning gleam:
　Sin' first I looked into her mother's face,
　All that dark time has left a strange, blurred trace.

71

She 'd caught some fever, doing angel's work
   Among the childer, down i' Hagalythe;
I like sometimes—set musing i' the mirk—
To think my winsome lassie gave her life
   Helping the helpless.   Well, the time flies past,
   The *Northern Star* has gone—I 'll follow fast.

   The best life left to me wer' spent wi' her
   'Mid the strange splendours i' them regions seen,
The great ice-plains wi' neither sound nor stir,
The mighty bergs, all blue, an' white, an' green,
   The plunging sea—the blowing of the whale—
   The flitting composants on shroud an' sail.

   I 've fancied, when in banners broad unfurled
   The crimson lights were glowing overhead,
As I could a'most see the other world,
Where Nance wer' waiting for me, parson said.
   Ay, many a year she 's borne us fast an' far,
   An' now she 's sold for firewood—poor auld *Star* !

   If I 'd the brass, I 'd buy the brave old boat,
   An' tak' her out, right out o' sight o' land,
An' scuttle her, as she lay there afloat—
I 've strength enow left in this shaking hand;
   An' so we 'd sink together, her an' me,
   To slumber to the hushing o' the sea.

   But that 's another idle dream—I 've got
   Enow to bury me by Nancy's side,
Up on the shelf there, i' the chiny pot,
She bade her mother gie me 'ere she died.
   I 'll try to beg a bit on t' *Star*, to make
   My coffin—for the last old whaler's sake.

SIR WILLIAM DOUGLAS

'SIR WILLIAM DOUGLAS'; nothing more, carved on
    the old grey stone,
Deep in the lush green boskage, by lichens over-
    grown.

'Sir William Douglas.' Quietly the good knight lies
    asleep,
Where the great oaks, like sentinels, their watch around
    him keep.

There, in the flush of spring-time, the primrose stars
    the grass,
And the wild birds on the hawthorn light, as to their
    nests they pass.

There in the golden summer eves the lingering lovers
    come,
And tell the sweet old story, as they rest beside his
    tomb.

There fall the leaves of autumn, all russet, gold, and
    red,
And, like a monarch's jewelled robe, bedeck his lonely
    bed.

And when the wind of winter the wood around him
rocks,

And deepens to an angry roar the babble of the
Brox,

Wide sweeping from their mountain-home, the whirl-
winds of the north

Lash into leaping, tossing foam the glittering waves of
Forth,

That crash upon the fair green Links, and thunder
faint and far,

Where from its height the massive Hold looks down
upon Dunbar.

Yet undisturbed the soldier lies, while the seasons
come and go,

While the roses laugh at Broxmouth, or the Lomonds
couch in snow.

And no man knows his story—if he fell in fray
forgot,

Where, in the wild hill-passes, Elliot met Kerr or
Scott ;

Or in the furious battle, where Dunse looks grimly
down,

Where on the storied plain below the Stuart staked
his crown ;

When, urged by fool and fanatic, brave Leslie left his
stand,

And Cromwell sternly smiled to see his foemen ' in his
hand.'

SIR WILLIAM DOUGLAS

Dying for king and country, as die a Douglas should?
None know, for very silently he lies in Broxmouth
    wood.

And only strangers tracking the ferny paths alone
Pause, to muse a wondering moment on a name, and
    on a stone.

THE THREE ANGELS

THE three great Angels by the Throne of Life
Honour, Unselfishness, and Sympathy;
Call on them, mortals, baffled in the strife,
Turn in thine anguish to the glorious Three;
Pure, true, and tender, clear as crystal is,
They will bring comfort in the place of bliss.

Sweeter are youth's fair spirits, Hope and Love;
But oh! they falter, change, and even die:
The Three alone, stern Time himself can prove,
Like steadfast stars they light the darkening sky,
Succour the failing hand, sustain the head,
Stand calm and strong beside the dying bed.

Honour will point the straight, unwavering way,
Unselfishness will quiet care and fret,
And Sympathy in low hushed accents say,
'The wound is deep, but balms await it yet.'
Fast falls the snow, keen blows the bitter blast;
The three great Angels lead us home at last.

A CHRISTMAS LETTER

How is it with you? The hot sunbeams shine
On you, amid the dazzling glow of flowers;
The luscious shadows of the trailing vine,
    The nature wealth that mocks this isle of ours,
Until the Christmas sunset redly stains
The long grey sweep of Australasian plains.

How is it with me? The thick snow-showers fall
    Outside my cottage by the northern sea,
The breakers thunder on the huge cliff wall,
    The east wind rushes o'er them fierce and free;
And misery's wail blends sadly with the roar
Of darkening billows crashing to the shore.

How many lonely Christmas days have gone
    Since we two parted, vowing, 'mid our tears,
To keep each other's troth till all was won,
    For which we parted 'a few short years'—
You, to go far to conquer time and fate,
I, to turn back beside the hearth and wait?

'A few short years!' I hardly care to glance
    At the poor face that now my mirror shows;
I shrink aside at the gay Christmas dance,
    I follow not where youth's light footstep goes.
And you are older, too; but then, one can
Forget grey hairs much better in a man.

A CHRISTMAS LETTER

And, looking now upon the yellowing heap
   Of letters, kept and read each Christmas over,
Somehow I fancy that the shadows creep
   Across the fervour of my brave young lover,—
The greetings that I write, as those you send,
Lack something of the first fresh warmth, my
    friend.

O yes, we keep, with somewhat over-care,
   Each sweet 'pet name,' each little 'customed
     phrase,
The golden coinage of the days that were,
   The April garland of the April days ;
Only, they ring a little forced, I think—
Forgive the woman's testing of the link !

And in the sacred name of Christmas, dear,
   By all the Past, by all the Future too,
Tell me the truth with neither shame nor fear,
   With steady hand the chain that galls undo ;
I shall be quite content, alone to pray
For him who gave my life its perfect day.

And if, so far away, the feverish strife
   For fame and gold was quite too much to bear,
Without one near and dear to bless your life,
   And you have found a 'Heartsease' blooming
     there ;
Give her to wear, for sake of our sweet folly,
On Christmas Day, this spray of English holly.

MORAY AND HIS THIRTY

MARCH 1313

LONG as the fair old city stands, the glory of the
    North,
Long as 'King Arthur's Seat' o'erlooks the flashing of
    the Forth;
Long as o'er lovely Edinbro' queens high her castled
    hold,
Of Moray and his Thirty shall the gallant tale be told.

St. Andrew's Cross was gleaming from many a taken
    wall,
As Highland isle and Lowland glen rose to the Bruce's
    call;
But from Stirling and from Edinbro', in firm defiance
    still,
The English Lion flaunted free and told her Sovereign's
    will.

Cold in his noble Abbey lay he whose sun had
    set
In clouds of stormy presage, the great Planta-
    genet;
'Mid favourites and fooleries, the weakly sapling lost
All that the mighty oak had won—won at such bitter
    cost.

But still King Edward's standard from the Castle floated
gay,
And still the rock impregnable held Bruce's best at bay,
To loyal threat and loyal strength laughed frank
defiance down,
Where Moray's baffled legions camped about the
subject town.

A soldier sought the warrior Earl, whose ready ear and
wit
Caught every rumour as it flew, and took the heart
from it ;
'I have scaled the rock full oft,' he said, 'in boyish
fear's despite :
Who is there, that for Bruce's sake, will try my path
to-night?

'O ay, the road is perilous, craves wary grasp and
tread,
And once a sentinel look down, by Mary, we were sped !
But the moon is at her birth, I wot, the clouds heap in
the west,
To dare and die—to dare and win—for Scotland, which
were best?'

'Right art thou,' fiery Moray said, and to his soldiers
spoke,
And, as they heard, an eager cry from every squadron
broke ;
Full many a stalwart trooper felt crossed hope was hard
to bear,
As Randolph chose his Thirty from the host of heroes
there.

The moon hung dim and haloed above the tossing
    Firth,
The wind swept with a muffled moan across the frost-
    bound earth ;
And from the driving wrack of clouds the light gleamed
    faint and far,
As, in black robes, the Thirty met round Moray's silver
    star.

High up in Edinbro' Castle, secure the English slept,
Their dreary rounds the sentinels in careful order
    stept ;
And creeping, struggling upwards, nerves, sinews, all
    astrain,
Clomb Randolph and his Thirty, their glorious prize to
    gain.

' Below there, ho ! I see you,' a soldier cried in
    jest ;
I trow the throbbing pulses froze in every warrior
    breast ;
Yet nor stir nor cry betokened their deadly peril when
The loosened crag came bounding down, 'mid Moray
    and his men.

Then rose the cry of wild surprise, of desperate dark-
    ling fight,
As, like ghosts, the bold invaders sprung upon that
    guarded height.
Brief was the furious struggle, as, startled from their
    rest,
Unarmed, amazed, the English met each fierce un-
    bidden guest.

And when the lingering morning broke upon the Castle
Rock,
The ruddy Lion ramped no more, the Scottish breeze
to mock ;
And when King Robert to his feast bid the captains of
his host,
'To Moray and his Thirty,' he pledged the crowning
toast.

'ÇA IRA'

1810

BEATEN backward in the press
Reeled the old Fourteenth;
And in triumph shrill arose
The yell of the triumphant foes,
As, where the British Lion flew,
Flaunted 'white, and red, and blue,'
For well the fiery Frenchmen knew
    The fame of the Fourteenth.

Beaten backward in the press
Reeled the old Fourteenth;
Cheerily their Colonel spoke,
As the red line round him broke;
Laughing, waving with his hand
To the leader of the band,
As again they took their stand,
    The men of the Fourteenth.

'Play the Frenchman's march,' he said,
The Chief of the Fourteenth;
'Strike it up—strike loud and clear;
As I stand before you here,
We will prove our mettle soon;
Ere yon pale sun rides at noon,
We'll beat them to their own brave tune,
    We men of the Fourteenth.'

'ÇA IRA'

Joyously the cheer arose
From the old Fourteenth ;
'Ça Ira !' gay and full and strong,
Rang the rallied ranks along ;
English hearts and steel were good ;
Rushing onwards like a flood,
Naught their furious charge withstood,
    The charge of the Fourteenth.

And they play 'Ça Ira' yet
    In the old Fourteenth ;
In memory of the glorious day
When they swept their foes away !
In memory of the right begun,
When, beneath the southern sun,
To the Frenchman's tune they won,
    The men of the Fourteenth.

LENT LILIES

Ay, it is over high for me to climb,
   Three hundred steps up to the Church-garth Head;
I say each year I hear the Easter chime,
   'Next time the mools will lie above my head.'
An' yet, for all I 've seen my eightieth year,
This bonnie morning finds me tottering here.

For I is loth that any other hand
   But mine should tend the lily-bed, you see;
For we were mates together on the land,
   An' mates on shipboard, allis, him an' me.
I likes to think he doesn't lie so deep,
But he can listen—just to hear me creep

Up to his headstone where the lilies blow,
   An' stand beside him while the church-bells ring.
Who was he? Why, it happened long ago,
   An' folks forget so; it 's a curious thing,
What I did yesterday seems far an' dim,
But I can mind all that, that chanced to him.

He sailed—let 's see, it 's sixty year agon—
   In the barque *Lecta*, bound for Elsinore,
An' I was vext that he took ship alone,
   While I was down wi' fever, here ashore;
But he says, 'Mate, I 'se need to keep my word,'
An' we shook hands, an' so he went aboard.

85

The master was a strange an' reckless man :
   He 'd sit and gloom for hours by the helm ;
An' when the hands were merry o'er the can,
   He 'd glower as he 'd fain ha' silenced them ;
An' when he 'd keep the watch, in all the barque,
None cared to stand aside him in the dark.

It was a Friday when the *Lecta* lay
   Safe back in Whitby Roads, an' sailors know
They must not make a port on such a day,
   Not though the winds moan and the glass runs low ;
Better ride out the wildest gale, they say,
Than on Black Friday try to make the Bay.

But little recked old Sam of freet or bode,
   He bade up anchor an' to fetch the port.
The men stood by the cable where she rode,
   An' moved with sullen foot, an' answered short.
One man stood out to cross the master's will,
One man alone, an' he my mate, our Bill.

How do I know it all ?   Well, wait a bit,
   I can't do to be harassed in a yarn—
It 's too much hurry ends in little wit,
   'Mid youngsters who can't tell thee stem frev starn.
Didn't old Sam come drifting safe ashore,
An' tell us all the log, from Elsinore?

He said our Bill stood up amid the crew,
   An' darred him to bring ruin on the lot.
Rough as he was, he gave the lad his due,
   An' to his death he never quite forgot
How he had thrust him back with heavy hand,
An' seized the helm, an' put her straight for land.

LENT LILIES

O' course she struck, out by the Black Nab yonder,
   An' parted amidships, an' one wild cry
Rang through the breakers' deep unceasing thunder,
   An' told its story to the darkening sky.
Old Sam made Saltwick, floating on a spar,
But all the rest lie drownded by the Scar—

All but my mate. Give us a light,—the tale
   Sounds queer, they say; but them as knows the coast,
Knows, too, of things to make their cheeks grow pale
   Who of theer land-larnt wisdom loudest boast;
I say, who knows it, sin' that fatal night,
Never a barque won past the Nab aright.

Something in loundest weather went across,
   A squall, a current, or a sudden wave;
Till, what with strange ill-luck, or wreck, or loss,
   A nameless fear that nigh turned back the brave,
An' made the coward useless—haunted like—
The Nab, that saw the *Lecta* drift an' strike.

An' soon a story grew, how, when the bells
   Rang out on Sabbath morns, a flitting shape
Glided where the white surf for ever swells,
   An' the great Nab shows like a rocky cape;
An' pointed downwards with a shadowy hand,
Where clinging weeds an' boulders strew the sand.

I, an' some more young chaps, went out to watch;
   The April day was rising sweet an' fair,
We saw the Scar the sun's first glitter catch,
   We saw the point, we saw the figure there;
An' as I looked I felt my heart stand still,
For in that awful thing I knew our Bill.

LENT LILIES

I loved the lad—I'd had to do a deal
  To keep hands off old Sam—an' when I saw
The poor hand motion dumb, I seemed to feel
  All that he wanted, that he meant to draw
Me on to do his work; an' like a shock
It came to me—he lay beneath the rock.

So next ebb-tide I found a chap as darred
  Heave with me at the boulders, one by one;
An' there we found him, lying torn an' scarred
  By wash of waves an' crash of shell an' stone.
But the old smile still showed as thof it met
The mate who strove to do his bidding yet.

We laid him in the Church-garth on the Head,
  With April sunshine dazzling on his grave;
An' a strange sort o' sigh, some old folk said,
  Went wailing out between the wind an' wave.
It might ha' been—I cannot justly say—
The devil moaned the curse wer' put away,

Sin' he who did his best to right a wrong
  Had fund at last a grave the parson blessed.—
My yarn has been above a bit too long.—
  I planted them Lent lilies by his rest:
For all you young 'uns grow so wise, 'twere well
To mind the warning that they bloom to tell:

For all that your black screaming steam can do,
  For all your charts to track the ocean way,
There's not a barque but has a cause to rue,
  Who on Black Friday venters from the Bay.
Yet, sin' our Bill lay safe in hallowed earth,
No need to give the Nab so wide a berth.

JUNE 21ST, 1879

LISTEN, great founder of the fated line,
Listen, in that right royal rest of thine,
Guarded by marshals, underneath the dome,
Where a repentant people bore thee home;
Above thy ashes pealed the triumphant gun,
That told how to thy house was born a son.
Can funeral echoes break thy rest to-day,
Because that son has passed from life away?
Because the last worst stroke of cruel fate
Has left the house thou foundest, desolate.

Listen, O pallid shade, whose birth to greet
All Europe crouched beneath thy father's feet:
Crowned King of Rome, in the brief brilliant hour,
That owned thee heir to the new Cæsar's power.
Poor sapling! crushed in the vast wreck around,
When the great oak came thundering to the ground;
To linger on as Fortune's toy and sport,
A slighted guest permitted at a court;
Too sad for effort, and too weak for strife,
Fading unmarked, unwept, away from life.

Listen, O sleeper, in the quiet grave,
That kindly England to the exile gave,
Where a pale shadow, once the loveliest queen
Imperial Paris in her pride has seen;

Beside her husband's dust must mourn alone
The child she trained to fill his father's throne;
Ah! lonely mothers, who blest vigil keep
Beside your rosy infant's guarded sleep,
You whose grey lines have got one centred joy,
How does a widow mourn her murdered Boy?

Listen! he comes, last, best of all his race,
Amid your ranks to claim an early place;
Happiest, perchance, of ye, the fated four,
Dying, ere trust was naught and hope was o'er;
Dying in savage war in Zululand,
Yet dying, face to foe and sword in hand,
Amid his chosen comrades' love and tears.
Snatched from the fret and fever of the years,
Honoured and mourned, the brave young hand has
    won
Meet laurels for the last Napoleon.

THE END

THE course of the weariest river
　　Ends in the great grey sea;
The acorn, for ever and ever,
　　Strives upward to the tree;
The rainbow the sky adorning
　　Shines promise through the storm;
The glimmer of coming morning
　　Through midnight gloom will form;
By time all knots are riven,
　　Complex although they be;
And peace will at last be given,
　　Dear, both to you and to me.

Then, though the path may be dreary,
　　Look onward to the goal:
Though the heart and the head be weary,
　　Let faith inspire the soul.
Seek the right, though the wrong be tempting;
　　Speak truth at any cost:
Vain is all weak exempting
　　When once that gem is lost.
Let strong hand and keen eye be ready
　　For plain or ambushed foes:
Thought earnest and fancy steady
　　Bear best unto the close.

THE END

The heavy clouds may be raining,
  But with evening comes the light ;
Through the dark are low winds complaining,
  Yet the sunrise gilds the height ;
And Love has his hidden treasure
  For the patient and the pure ;
And Time gives his fullest measure
  To the workers who endure ;
And the Word that no love has shaken
  Has the future pledge supplied ;
For we know that when we 'awaken,'
  We shall be 'satisfied.'

COME BACK

ONLY come back, to say that you forget
   The foolish, angry words I said that day;
To heal the aching of the long regret,
    To hear the lips all that they said, unsay;
       Only come back!

Dear, I would be so gentle and so sweet,
   Would tread so duteously the very track
Where you had planned untiring steps should meet;
       Only come back!

I would forgo all little things I thought
   Made full life's purpose. What of life could lack,
If sacrifice of all your presence bought?
       Only come back!

Only come back! Indeed I loved you, dear;
   Indeed we loved each other. Ah, your eyes,
Free from all earth-clouds, see it, full and clear;
    Watching in pitying patience from the skies;
       Only come back!

A REST

WHEN the fret and the fever is over,
  When no longer we struggle and grieve,
When the kind daisied turfs are laid over
  The poor tirèd clay that we leave;
When life offers no prize for the gaining,
  When the hope has gone out of the quest,
Done with planning and yearning and straining,
  For us there remaineth a rest.

The hand grows so weary of fighting,
  The heart of the idols that break;
The eyes are too dim for delighting
  In the fair things that fancy may make;
Trust pierces the bosom so often;
  Love is but a toy at the best,
Yet has stings that no patience can soften—
  For us there remaineth a rest.

When faith has proved all unavailing,
  And earthly hopes vanish away,
Ah! why should the frail and the failing
  In the world that has naught for them stay?
This balm is stored up for their aiding,
  The weary and worn and distressed,
When the last gleam of life's light is fading,
  For them there remaineth a rest.

CANCELLING

When the kind eyes are closed, the sweet lips dumb,
  And cold to our wild kisses lies the Dead;
When we add, helplessly, the cruel sum
  Of careless things we did, harsh words we said,
When but to blot the bitter record out,
  But to unsay, undo, repent, recall,
To be forgiven wrong, or jar, or doubt,
  Were worth, of life's remaining prizes, all.

What hurts the sorest? tears we caused to flow?
  Hours that we clouded? days we might have blest?
Trifles that only now we seem to know,
  So hardly on the gentle spirit pressed?
Nay, all of these, in this our vain remorse,
  Encompass us, each with their separate stings;
But, worst of all, in their o'erwhelming force,
  Are memories of tender cancellings.

The tardy, graceless vows of late repentance,
  How eagerly and tenderly they heard!
What fond forgiveness met the broken sentence,
  As the soft kiss silenced the faltering word!
O quiet lips that pardoned! folded fingers
  That clasped a half-reluctant hand of yore!
What pain like his, as by his Dead he lingers,
  Knowing she'll cancel fault or wrong no more!

THE DAY'S WORK

Do thy day's work, my dear,
Though fast and dark the clouds are drifting near,
Though time has little left for hope and very much for
   fear.

Do thy day's work, though now
The hand must falter and the head must bow,
And far above the failing foot shows the bold mountain
   brow.

Yet there is left for us,
Who on the valley's verge stand trembling thus,
A light that lies far in the west—soft, faint, but
   luminous.

We can give kindly speech,
And ready helping hands to all and each,
And patience, to the young around, by smiling silence
   teach.

We can give gentle thought,
And charity, by life's long lesson taught,
And wisdom, from old faults lived down, by toil and
   failure wrought.

THE DAY'S WORK

We can give love, unmarred
By selfish snatch at happiness, unjarred
By the keen aims for power, or joy, that make youth
    cold and hard.

And if gay hearts reject
The gifts we hold—would fain fare on unchecked
On the bright roads that scarce yield all that young eyes
    expect,—

Why, do thy day's work still.
The calm, deep founts of love are slow to chill;
And Heaven may yet the harvest yield, the work-worn
    hands to fill.

JULY 12TH, 1896

'To absent Friends,' we drank to-night.
Outside, the lingering northern light
Lay softly over loch and lea,
While the huge crown of Benachie
Rose royally in purple might.

Inside, the wine-cup sparkled bright,
And with her dark eyes shining, she
Said that our Sunday toast must be
'To absent Friends.'

The touch struck the heart-cords aright,
And as each pledged it silently,
Our thoughts flew far o'er land and sea,
And to some passed from human sight.
Ah, well! next Sunday think of me,
With absent friends.

'LOVE THE GIFT, IS LOVE THE DEBT'

'LOVE the gift, is love the debt,'
Take the lesson, sweetly set,
O cold youth! to whom love's boon
Comes as roses do in June,
Fresh and fragrant, lightly won
By the kisses of the sun;
Blooming equally for all,
In wild or parterre, cot or hall.

Take the gift so freely given
As the richest under heaven;
It will light the darkest day,
It will smooth the roughest way;
Hush the sigh, recall the smile,
Full and patient all the while,
Only, never quite forget,
'Love the gift, is love the debt.'

For a dreadful day will come,
When eyes are dim and lips are dumb,
Or love reluctantly may turn
From the hearts that proudly spurn;
Wearied of the chill reply,
Of the happy hours let by,
Of baffled yearning, vain regret:
'Love the gift, is love the debt.'

99

Then in full the tribute pay,
Give the pittance while you may ;
Blossoms droop and sunbeams fade,
Of the dark hours be afraid ;
Lest some day you vainly plead
For help and strength in bitter need ;
Think, when hope and faith are met,
' Love the gift, is love the debt.'

THE LAST WISH

Just that the last face I shall see
As the world grows dim and dazed to me;
Just that the last voice I shall hear,
As all grows hushed to the dulling ear;
Just that the last clasp I shall feel,
As the chills of death around me steal;—
That yours is smile, and tone, and touch,
Darling, Love asks of Life so much.

Since surely in its last long bed
Content would lie the weary head,
If One, the best beloved of life,
Stood by to aid its parting strife;
Ah, Lord of hope, and will, and breath,
Your empire cannot cease with death;—
Do thou my latest prayer and trust,
Love still will bless thee from the dust.

HEARTSEASE

Where shall we seek for Heartsease?—we who fain
  That precious thing would gain?
Dearer than love, since love may change or die;
Dearer than fame, that like a flash goes by;
The richest gift that, since the world began,
  God gave to man.

Not in the fret and fever of the strife
  Of busy onward life,
Not in the passionate conflicts of the heart,
Not in the lovely cultured world of art,
Not in the cloistered student's living tomb,
  Will Heartsease bloom.

But in the sober twilight's quiet time,
  When to the evening chime
The tired pilgrim walks with patient feet,
Willing the tasks he yet can do to meet,
Content with all Heaven portions as his share—
  Seek Heartsease there.

BY THE YEW-HEDGE

Up and down the terrace pacing, where the winter sun-
    light glowed,
And the sound of falling waters timed my footsteps as
    I trode,
Pacing where the tall yew-hedges kept the bitter blast
    away,
And the noontide smiled like summer on the January
    day.

Up and down the terrace pacing, for a musing hour
    alone,
While the river's music mingled with the baffled east
    wind's moan,
And a presence seemed beside me, very close and very
    dear,
A strong hand my hand was clasping, a low voice was
    in my ear.

Words of counsel, words of comfort, words of dear
    companionship,
And the blue eyes spoke as softly as the mobile eager
    lip ;
Hope grew brighter, grief grew sweeter, doubt, ashamed,
    shrank quiet away,
As we two paced on together, in the January day.

Swift and sweet the moments passed me, as the sun-
    shine paled o'erhead,
And, to common life returning, fell the slow, reluctant
    tread ;
Yet my hushed heart from its commune, patience,
    strength, and courage drew ;
And north skies with southern splendour gilded all
    the darkling yew.

'A LA JOUR, LA JOURNÉE'

A LA jour, la journée: what does it avail
In the lightly chequered sky to read the coming gale?
We cannot check its fury, we cannot chain its wing,
Nor stay the deadly ruin its loosened might may bring;
To-day the day is balmy, to-day the sun shines bright,
A la jour, la journée, reck not of the night.

A la jour, la journée: the wisdom of the old
Says, once the prize is captured, the hunter's warmth
    grows cold,
The voice will lose its fervour, the hand its clinging
    clasp,
As the fair flower that hung so high droops in the
    victor's grasp.
Well, now the kiss is passionate; the smile is tender
    now,
A la jour, la journée, trust the lover's vow.

A la jour, la journée: age creeps slow and sure,
Where youth's frank laugh is ringing, where youth's
    first joys are pure,
Season follows season, stealing one by one,
April's promise, July's rose, October's sober sun;
Change, weariness, satiety, each pleasure follows fast,
A la jour, la journée, prize them while they last.

A la jour, la journée : He who rules it all,
He who loved the lilies, and saw the sparrow fall,
Sends the sorrows, metes the joy, gives the golden hour,
Appoints the bitter healing frost, sows or blights the
    flower ;
He knows each footstep on the way, so weakly, blindly
    trod,
A la jour, la journée, leave the rest to God.

WHERE?

WHERE are the blossoms of April?
　Where are the roses of June?
Where is the passionate gladness
　That thrilled in the rivulet's tune?

Around us the autumn is drooping,
　The snow and the frost follow soon;
Where are the blossoms of April?
　Where are the roses of June?

The red leaves about us are drifting,
　The sun does but shimmer at noon;
How it flitted and flashed in our April!
　What glory it gave us in June!

Where is the magic of starlight,
　The mystical lore of the moon?
Gone with the blossoms of April,
　Gone with the roses of June.

HAPPINESS

Happiness, the white bird that seldom lights;
　　We hear her calling from her hidden caves,
We see her flashing in her sudden flights
　　Over the gladness of the sunlit waves;
Flashing, with morning's glory on her wings,
　　Flashing, with youth's frank vigour on her way,
We see her, queen of our imaginings,
　　But who amongst us that can bid her stay?

We hear her music ringing through the dawn,
　　We hear it murmuring in the noonday hush,
We hear it softest when the day withdrawn
　　Leaves the warm earth to sunset's lingering blush;
But would we track the songstress to her nest,
　　Swift as the breeze that bears her, she is gone,
Bearing away with her our first and best,
　　Leaving us in a dark'ning world alone.

Better to rest content with what we have,
　　Glimpse of her beauty, echo of her voice;
Nor for the full abiding presence crave,
　　That bids so seldom life on earth rejoice:
And ye, who for a golden moment cage
　　The white immortal bird, that moment prize
To grace the youth, to sanctify the age,
　　Until ye find her dwelling, in the skies.

GUESTS

To my door in the summer gloaming
   Three lordly strangers came;
Each paused a moment by me,—
   They were Friendship, Love, and Fame.

Each said in his gracious staying,
   That on the roll he held
He would trace my name for ever.
   I heard them, spirit-spelled.

Fame carried a block of marble,
   And Friendship a vellum white;
Love bore a waxen tablet,
   His fingers touched to light.

Ere half my name was carven,
   Glory had left my side;
Love laughed, as he saw each letter,
   As he graved it, glowed, and died.

But Friendship on her parchment
   The name of my bright youth set,
And though my eyes grow dim with years,
   I can read it traced there yet.

REQUIESCAT

ONE frail bark the less on the billow,
One actor dropt out of the play,
One tired head more on the pillow,
One toiler the less on the way.

The hand was too feeble for labour,
The head was too heavy for thought ;
If they looked round for friend or for neighbour,
The dim eyes scarce found what they sought.

For the call, never ceasing from sounding,
Thins the ranks with each moment that flies ;
The world of our gay youths surrounding,
Is less in the earth than the skies.

Then lay the green turf sods above him,
Place the cross that he served o'er his breast,
Say, nearest of those left to love him :
'It is well for the weary at rest.'

ANEMONES

It was a happy holiday of ours,
When first we trod the sunny southern shore !
'Twas the poor patch of closely tended flowers
I saw, this moment, through the hothouse door,
That sent my fancy flying o'er the seas,
To that bright day we saw Anemones—

Saw them in glory, do you recollect?
Or are the trackless plains of Heaven too fair
To care how richly, royally, they decked
The mountain-side, as we stood lingering there,
Happy in wonder, beauty, love—we two?
How much of all has passed from life with you !

Above us shone the bright Italian sun,
Below, the ' city of the golden shell,'
Around, the haunts we knew when life begun,
Through the old pages that we loved so well;
And all about us, sky, and hill, and sea,
Lay in the glory that was—Sicily.

And spreading far adown the mountain-side,
The flashing masses of the flowers sprung;
And as we looked from where, in marble pride,
She 'mid her jewels lay, who died so young ;
Down Pellegrino swept the scented breeze,
And ' Look,' you said, ' at the Anemones !'

ANEMONES

How all the crimson living lustre swayed,
Like rosy billows on the ocean swell;
Then tossed their fairy heads as if they made
A voiceless music from each fragile bell;
Till, dazzled by their glow, we turned away.
Have you forgotten, dear, that crowning day?

Forgotten our sweet month of wandering?
Forgotten our long life of flawless love?
Forgotten our slow parting's bitter sting,
In the blessed waiting of the life above?
They are but English blooms I train to wave
Beside the northern seaboard, on your grave.

JUDGED

YES, while he lived he was foolish !
  Half-vexed, half-amused, we have heard
The trouble that rose about trifles,
  The weight we would give to a word !
We had thought it were idle to listen
  To the querulous warnings he said,
To his doubt, to his dream, to his omen—
  But now he is dead.

And something came out of the silence,
  The terrible silence that fell
Round the pause in the feeble existence,
  Whose weakness we all knew so well ;
Just as on the face, slight and quiet,
  A strange, awful beauty was shed,
That deepened each hour we watched him—
  Now that he was dead.

We remembered quick answer and slighting,
  We remembered each laugh and each frown,
As on the cold face and crossed fingers
  We stood looking solemnly down ;
And the smile on the pale lips that rested,
  Seemed, as if that he could, he had said :
' My mourners have learned a strange reverence—
  Because I am dead.'

H   113

JUDGED

Ah, patience and charity, brothers,
    Let us learn them before 'tis too late ;
Not all have the same high ideal,
    Not all can be steadfast and great ;
The narrowest man, or the coldest,
    By his own hidden light may be fed.
' Judge not.' Each harsh judgment will sting us—
    The Judged lying dead.

A THOUGHT

THAT just a pausing pulse, a ceasing breath,
   May stop for ever joys, and hopes, and fears ;
   And all the gathering tumult of the years
Sink in an instant to the hush of death !

It is a thought one does not realise,
   Whatever are the 'customed words we say ;
   So steady seems our hold on every day,
And life as certain as the change of skies.

Only sometimes, in a strange helplessness,
   We feel, ' And will to-morrow dawn for us ? '
   And close our eyes in dumb reliance thus,
Though all before us narrows to a guess.

There would be some amaze—some tears would fall,
   Some lives be darkened for a little space,
   And then the waves sweep o'er the vacant place.
And yet we live, we are, and God knows all !

ONLY A DREAM

ONLY a dream, my darling,
A dream as false and fair !
How it shone in the blossoming flowers,
How it breathed in the wooing air !
It woke with the rising morning,
It blushed in the sunset gleam ;
It shed its radiance on the way,
It brightened the hours of every day,
And oh ! there was never a voice to say,
    Only a dream !

Only a dream, my darling ;
We were both in earnest, too,
And every word we whispered
And every glance was true.
How could we know that promise
So rich and strong could seem,
Yet die as the frail fair lilies die
When the east winds mock the April sky ?
We thought it eternal, you and I—
    Only a dream !

THE DEATH OF LOVE

AND is he dead at last? He lingered long,
Despite the fever-fits of doubt and pain;
It seemed that faith had wov'n a web so strong,
'Twould keep him till his pulse beat true again.
Centre of so much youth, and hope, and trust,
How could he crumble into common dust?

Cold blew the icy winds of circumstance;
Prudence and penury stood side by side,
Barbing the arrow shot by crafty chance,
Snatching the balsam from the wounds of pride;
Slander spiced well the cup false friendship gave,
And so Love died. Where shall we make his grave?

Scatter no roses on the bare black earth,
Plant no white lilies, no blue violet bloom.
Weak in his death, as feeble in his birth,
Why should life strive to sanctify his tomb?
Even gentle memory is by truth forbid
To honour aught that died as light Love did.

Let the rank grasses flourish fearlessly,
With no fond footsteps brushing them away;
While the young life he troubled, strong and free,
Turns to the promise of the world's new day,
Leaving the darkening skies to close above
The unhallowed burial-place of shallow Love.

THE ROSARY

I HAVE strung them on a golden string,
  Those dated days of ours ;
Like diamond stars is their glittering,
  Their perfume like summer flowers ;
And when I sit in the dusk alone,
  When the long 'day's darg' is over and done,
I take my Rosary from its nest,
  Hidden warmly away in my breast,
And tell my beads with a lingering touch,
  My beads that recall and mean so much,
And live again through each little thing,
  Of the past and its precious dowers ;
Through the tears and the smiles that ever cling
  Around our sweet past hours.

I gathered them softly one by one
  From Memory's borderland,—
Some lay full in the noonday sun,
  And some nestled deep in sand.
Some were o'ergrown by the verdant turf,
  And some lay tumbled amid the surf
That chafes for ever upon the shore,
  Where Time is breathing, 'No more ; no more,'
And some were set so hard in frost,
  That Hope shrank from them as something lost;

THE ROSARY

But Love smiled down from his stand,
    And watched till my task was done,
As I strung them with soft and tender hand,
    The treasures my search had won.

Oh, cruel time and tide may do
    Full many a bitter deed,
Since all that we may plead and rue
    Cannot check or change their speed.
Much we may dream of, much we may trust,
    Will fade, like the rose of a day, to dust ;
The hope we cherished may sigh and part,
    The reed we leant on may pierce the heart :
But nothing can dim the tender shine
    Clinging about these jewels of mine ;
And never in vain, for me or for you,
    Can Memory's magic plead,
For pure and rounded, rich and true,
    Is every threaded bead !

FRIENDS

‘ FRIENDS ! I count them by scores,’ said eager Youth,
  ’Mid his April joy-bells’ chime ;
‘ I will stake my all on their faith and truth,’
  And he laughed in the face of Time.
But Change stood near, and close he clasped
  The hand of Satiety :
‘ I bide my hour, I know my power—
  What is Friendship, matched with me ?’

‘ Friends ! I have them close and true,’
  Said Manhood in his prime ;
‘ I prize what I’ve proved in measure due,’
  And proudly he looked on Time.
But Fate and Fortune grimly smiled,
  A smile that was ominous :
‘ Who will count the cost when the game is lost ?
  What are earth’s ties to us ? ’

‘ Friends ! I have one that still will bide
  By my hearth till midnight chime,’
Age, with a wistful, troubled pride,
  Muttered to threatening Time.
But as he spoke he shivered
  As struck by an icy breath,
‘ Ay, one I will leave, too old to grieve,
  Said the slow, cold tones of Death.

FRIENDS

'Friends!' and the student, as he spoke,
    Glowed with a fire sublime,
And a triumph light in his blue eyes woke,
    As he smiled, supreme, at Time:
'My books charm manhood and quiet youth,
    And the friends that they have given,
From the loaded shelves, a world in themselves,
    Soothe Age, and point to Heaven.'

DOOMED!

BETTER a sudden wrench than slow decay—
What boots to linger by the open tomb?
What boots to shrink before the creeping gloom?
Nor strife nor prayer the certain hour can stay;
Sure as the night comes to the brightest day,
The feeble, fainting love must dree its doom,
Though Faith its likeness may a while assume,
Or Hope its lingering agony delay.
Better clasp hands and part, while yet we hold
The golden links unsnapped—not wait to see
The fatal canker of satiety
Eat through the ore that was so pure of old;
The glamour pales, the pulse beats sad and slow—
My darling, kiss me once, and let me go!

A TANGLED WEB

A TANGLED web ! and all it wants
Is just what Fortune never grants :
An eye with pure, undazzled sight,
A steady hand to part aright
The crossing threads that twist and blend,
And hold asunder friend from friend ;
While lovers 'mid their broken dreams,
Their baffled hopes, their thwarted schemes,
Know, amid tears, and loss, and fall,
The tangled web has spoilt it all !

The tangled web !—a hasty kiss,
A careless word marked all amiss,
A clasp too short, a glance too long,
An idle word, a passionate song ;
Too little said, too much implied,
And man's light faith, and woman's pride ;
A lack of honest trust and truth,
The quick despair of eager youth,
And two lives wrecked beyond recall,—
The tangled web has spoilt it all !

AUTUMN LEAVES

FALLING, ever falling,
  To the west wind's sighs ;
Falling, ever falling,
  'Neath November skies,
From great forest monarchs,
  From clustered cottage eaves,
From arbour, hedge, and trellis-walk,
  Drift the autumn leaves.

Leaves our sweetest poet
  In stormy spring-tide sung ;
Leaves our noblest painter
  Drew when all were young.
Gems the poorest gather,
  Gauds the simplest see,
Heaped in golden glow and gleam,
  Under every tree.

Russet, brown, and crimson,
  Rustling where we tread,
Over sweeping uplands
  In rich profusion shed ;
Shining where the sunlight
  Faintly flickers down,
Giving dying Nature's head
  A fantastic crown.

AUTUMN LEAVES

Falling as our hopes do
    When our winter nears us,
Glittering as our dreams do
    When fond fancy cheers us;
Harvest that the parting year
    Gathers, as she grieves,
To strew o'er her dead darling, June,
    Drift the autumn leaves.

THE OLD PHRASE

THE sweet old phrase, you use it still,
And loyally you strive to make
Your voice the olden music take—
Your voice that disobeys your will.

No, sweetheart, no ; the fire is chill,
It does but deepen yet the ache,
The sweet old phrase.

What use the custom to fulfil,
When not for even old sake's sake,
All that the words once meant will wake?
Leave it laid very cold and still,
The sweet old phrase.

COST-COUNTING

Love, do you ever think how strange it is,
How the bonds loosen, how the links decay,
How slow and sure it vanishes away,
The dream we thought would make our all of bliss?
We speak, a little carelessly, each phrase
We loved so jealously a year ago;
We have not swerved a step aside, you know,
From the old rose-encircled fairy ways;
Yet you and I both feel the game is done—
Counting the cost is always left for one.

And—women are so—I am glad that I
The bitter, necessary work should take;
Time cannot ask of you, that for my sake,
You need look backwards with a wistful sigh.
Each word you said, each smile you gave, was true,
'Tis life, and fate, that cut our bond in twain.
I love you so, I cherish e'en the pain,
That leaves me something yet, as dealt by you.
Rich was the gift your lavish nature gave,
And I, and memory, will guard its grave.

'WHEN WE WERE YOUNG'

When we were young, how softly played
Sweet April's charm of shine and shade!
How rich and red the rose of June,
How royal was the Autumn boon,
What jovial mirth old Winter made!

How light the breeze on glen and glade,
When down the moorland paths we strayed,
To listen to the streamlets' tune!
When we were young.

Ah! happy magic passed too soon,
When life sang Nature's guileless rune;
Where love or sunshine ever stayed,
Of falsehood or of frost afraid.
Did east winds mock the sweet May moon,
When we were young?

THE LAST ROSE

THE last red rose low droops its head,
Where all her sister petals shed,
As rich and rare as hers of old,
Lie on the black, unlovely mould,
Fair sleepers for so rough a bed,
And the fierce east wind raves, frost-fed,
From mountain passes, drear and dread,
And threatens with the coming cold
    The last red rose.

' I mourn not that my time has fled,'
Soft to the wind the blossom said,
   ' As summer hours their warmth unrolled,
My story to sweet youth I told,
Now, age may shrine my fragrance dead ;
    The last red rose.'

AJAR

THE tiny grain of sand arrests the wheel,
  The note that falsely rings spoils all the air;
The drop of poison through the draught will steal,
  And leave its work of hidden murder there.

The erring touch the perfect picture blurs,
  The careless smile may sting a hope to death;
A pebble flung the lake's whole surface stirs,
  The troubled waters crush a root beneath.

And a rash-written word, or spoken jest,
  May stop affection's fountain at its source,
Or kill a love that warmed a human breast,
  And in its stead leave the grim ache—remorse.

THE DAISY

She put it among my laces, the Daisy that never dies,
The child with June roses in her cheeks, and her
   mother in her eyes ;
The tiny fingers carefully placing the muslin thing,
Till I thought the dews, the spring morns use, on its
   leaves were glistening.

For childhood's sunny halo, and April's golden air,
Clung round the poor, pale, paltry toy, the Baby brought
   me there ;
And I felt the phantoms of the past from their old
   graves arise,
As with a kiss she gave me this, ' the Daisy that never
   dies.'

Soft lips that my blood has reddened, blue eyes that
   her mother had,
When she brought the best sweet crown of joy to the
   life grown grey and sad ;
What though the sunset reddens low in the gloaming
   skies,
She brings a light to the closing night, with the Daisy
   that never dies.

LOVE

My love is steadfast as its source is pure ;
My love is glorious as its source is bright ;
My love, as seeking not its own delight,
But rather her sweet safety to ensure,
Her gladness in life's turmoils to secure,
   Is fitted so to meet the angels' sight,
   Who hover round her fair head day and night.
Strong as the Heaven that guards her to endure,
Darling, my stream of fate may ebb and flow,
   May flash in sunshine, or go down in gloom ;
   So nothing touch thy soft unruffled bloom,
Or mar the sweet serene I worship so.
   Only give this, my one sufficient need,
   Saying, ' Such love as his was love indeed.'

GOOD NIGHT

GOOD NIGHT, my love ! Serene and still
The moonlight sleeps upon the hill ;
Like sentinels the giant trees
Stand stately on the silvered leas.
I hear the tinkle of the rill,

I hear the rich delicious trill
Of nightingales the silence fill ;
I hear the sound of distant seas.
Good night, my love !

I call my pulse, and sense, and will,
My heart's fond bidding to fulfil ;
I join my spirit-voice to these ;
I whisper to the wandering breeze,
That breathes around me soft and chill :
Good night, my love !

Printed by T. and A. Constable, Printers to Her Majesty
at the Edinburgh University Press

PUBLICATIONS & ANNOUNCE-
MENTS OF MR. GRANT RICHARDS
AT No. 9 HENRIETTA STREET
COVENT GARDEN, LONDON

Spring
1898

BOOKS NOW READY, ARRANGED IN ORDER OF PRICE

35s. net.

English Portraits.

20s. net.

Evolution of the Idea of God.

10s. 6d.

H.R.H. The Prince of Wales.

7s. 6d.

In Court and Kampong.

6s.

True Heart.
Wheel of God.
Cattle Man.
Aunt Judith's Island.
Actor-Manager.
Studies in Brown Humanity.
Linnet.
Wooings of Jezebel Pettyfer.
Ape, the Idiot, and other People.
Yellow Danger.
Blastus.
Logic : Deductive and Inductive.
African Millionaire.
"Old Man's" Marriage.
Book of Verses for Children.
Flower of the Mind.
Laughter of Jove.

5s. net.

Hannibal.
Porphyrion.
Versions from Hafiz.
Inferno of Dante.
St. Botolph.
Pioneers of Evolution.
Limbo.
Poems by A. and L.

5s.

Plays : Pleasant and Unpleasant.
Bishops of the Day.
Cakes and Ale.
Real Ghost Stories.
Old Rome and the New.
Tom, Unlimited.
Rubaiyat of Omar Khayyam.

3s. 6d. net.

The Wind in the Trees.
Grant Allen's Guides.
Spikenard.
Hernani.

3s. 6d.

Convict 99.
Where Three Creeds Meet.
Little Stories about Women.
One Man's View.
Paul's Stepmother.
Subconscious Self.
Tenth Island.

3s. net.

Realms of Unknown Kings :
  Buckram.
Politics in 1896.

2s. 6d. net.

Tabulation of the Factory Laws.
Aglavaine and Selysette.
English Portraits : Parts.

2s. 6d.

Ethics of Browning's Poems.
Peakland Faggot.

2s. net.

New Zealand.
Realms of Unknown Kings :
  Paper.

2s.

Letters from Julia.
Ethics of the Surface Series.
Cub in Love : Cloth.

1s. 6d.

Dumpy Books.
Cub in Love : Paper.

1s.

Labour in the Longest Reign.

ANNOUNCEMENTS

∾ ∾ ∾

A new volume will be added to Mr. GRANT ALLEN'S series of Historical Guides.

Venice

Three volumes in the series have already appeared, PARIS, FLORENCE, and CITIES OF BELGIUM; and ROME and CITIES OF NORTHERN ITALY are in preparation. Of the general need for the series, the Morning Post *says :—*

"That much-abused class of people, the tourists, have often been taunted with their ignorance and want of culture, and the perfunctory manner in which they hurry through, and 'do' the Art Galleries of Europe. There is a large amount of truth, no doubt, but they might very well retort on their critics that no one had come forward to meet their wants, or assist in dispelling their ignorance. No doubt there are guide-books, very excellent ones in their way, but on all matters of art very little better than mere indices ; something fuller was required to enable the average man intelligently to appreciate the treasures submitted to his view. Mr. Grant Allen has offered to meet their wants, and offers these handbooks to the public at a price that ought to be within the reach of every one who can afford to travel at all. The idea is a good one, and should ensure the success which Mr. Allen deserves."

Grant Allen's Historical Guides are bound in green cloth, with rounded corners, to slip into the pocket. Fcap. 8vo. 3s. 6d. each, net.

3

New Fiction

BY FREDERIC BRETON

Author of "The Black Mass," "The Trespasses of Two," etc.

True Heart

Being Passages in the Life of Eberhard Treuherz,
Scholar and Craftsman, telling of his Wanderings
and Adventures, his Intercourse with People
of Consequence to their Age, and how
he came scatheless through a
Time of Strife

While doing his best to retain ample romantic interest,
Mr. Breton's intention has been to present a true picture of
the time rather than to produce a mere novel of incident.

In One Volume, 6s.

BY GEORGE EGERTON

Author of "Keynotes," "Discords," etc.

The Wheel of God

Hitherto "George Egerton's" books have been made
up of short stories. "The Wheel of God" is her first long
novel, and deals with woman's life both in America and in
England. Its note is one rather of reaction than of revolt.

In One Volume, 6s.

BY G. B. BURGIN

Author of "'Old Man's' Marriage," "Tuxter's Little Maid," etc.

The Cattle Man

In One Volume, 6s.   [*Ready.*

4

New Fiction

BY LEONARD MERRICK

Author of "One Man's View," "Cynthia," etc.

The Actor-Manager

Mr. Merrick writes of theatrical life in London and the provinces from a fulness of knowledge : he has been both actor and dramatist. His story here is that of an actor's progress, social and artistic, and of the clash of ideas with the hard necessity of the box-office.

In One Volume, 6s.

◝ ◝

BY HUGH CLIFFORD

Author of "In Court and Kampong."

Studies in Brown Humanity

Being Scrawls and Smudges in Sepia, White, and Yellow

Mr. Hugh Clifford, who occupies the important post of British Resident at Pahang in the Malay Peninsula, achieved considerable success with his first book, "In Court and Kampong," of which this book is in some sense a continuation, dealing as it does with the tragic, eventful lives of the varied peoples among whom lies his work.

" The chief aim is to portray character, to reveal to the European thoughts, passions, and aspirations which unfold themselves but slowly even to him who for long years has lived the life of his Asiatic associates in places remote from the sound of western civilisation. . . . In this effort Mr. Clifford has achieved a considerable success ; and as he writes also in a bright style, which has a distinctly literary flavour, his work is not less welcome for the information which it gives than interesting as a story-book."—*Athenæum* on "In Court and Kampong."

In One Volume, 6s.

◝ ◝

BY GRANT ALLEN

Linnet : a Romance

The story of a Tyrolese peasant-girl who becomes a great singer. The scenes are laid in the Tyrol, in London, Monte Carlo, and elsewhere : the treatment varying between the idyllic and the novel of society.

In One Volume, 6s. [*June.*

5

𝕹𝖊𝖜 𝕱𝖎𝖼𝖙𝖎𝖔𝖓

BY MARIE AND ROBERT LEIGHTON

Convict 99
A True Story of Penal Servitude

With 8 Full-page Illustrations by STANLEY L. WOOD.
In One Volume, 3s. 6d.

❧ ❧

BY HALDANE MACFALL

The Wooings of Jezebel Pettyfer
*Being the Personal History of Jehu Sennacherib Dyle,
Commonly called Masheen Dyle*

A realistic story of West Indian negro life, written with sympathy
and knowledge, Mr. Macfall having held, for a considerable period, a
commission in a West Indian regiment. "He has aimed at giving
us," says *The Literary World* in an advance note on the book, "negro
views of life, negro religious prejudices, and negro superstitions. The
hero is a Zouave, and the chief characters are negroes—acting and
living like negroes—and not, as in most books of the kind, travesties
of the white man."
In One Volume, 6s.

❧ ❧

BY DR. J. CAMPBELL OMAN

Where Three Creeds Meet
A Tale of Indian Life
In One Volume, 3s. 6d.

❧ ❧

BY W. T. STEAD

Blastus, the King's Chamberlain

A reprint, with a new introduction of considerable length, of an old
Christmas number of the *Review of Reviews*, long out of print. In the
tale, Mr. Stead made the experiment of prophesying the immediate
future of a prominent politician whose identity is only thinly veiled.
Events have given that prophecy an extreme interest, which Mr. Stead's
new introduction greatly enhances.

In One Volume, 6s.

6

New Fiction

By W. C. MORROW

The Ape, the Idiot, and other People

Mr. Morrow, an American, has produced here a collection of short stories of the weird, the horrible, and the grotesque, reminding us now of Robert Louis Stevenson, now of Edgar Allan Poe, and now of Mr. H. G. Wells, but retaining at the same time a note of his own that is likely to make his volume a considerable success.

In One Volume, 6s.

❧ ❧

By M. P. SHIEL

Author of " Prince Zaleski," etc.

The Yellow Danger

The plot of this story is laid in the present year, the first chapters dealing with those incidents in the Far East that have so fluttered the chancelleries of the West. A great leader—half Chinese, half Japanese—unites the yellow races, and conceives the idea of setting the nations of Europe at war by giving to the three great Continental powers vast tracts of Chinese land. The policy of the " open door " forces England to fight the coalition, and, as a result, the object of the East is achieved—Europe is decimated and enfeebled, lying open to the locust swarm of the yellow races (the " Yellow Danger " of the *Spectator*). And then—then England saves the world. Although dealing with so vast a subject, there is no lack of personal interest and individual incident in Mr. Shiel's work.

In One Volume, 6s.

❧ ❧

By F. C. CONSTABLE

Author of " The Curse of Intellect."

Aunt Judith's Island
A Comedy of Kith and Kin

A satirical novel of society and European politics. In Aunt Judith the author has added to that gallery of resourceful women (which already is graced by Mrs. Poyser and Betsy Trotwood, Gainor Wynne, Old Pummeloe, and Mrs. Major O'Dowd) a millionaire with pronounced views on Socialism and enough opportunism to stock three Prime Ministers. How Aunt Judith reconciles the various branches of her family, and conducts the Concert of Europe, one must read the story to discover.

In One Volume, 6s.

7

Drama

By GEORGE BERNARD SHAW

Plays : Pleasant and Unpleasant

I. Unpleasant. II. Pleasant.

With special Portrait in photogravure of the Author.

The existence of a number of unpublished and unperformed plays by Mr. Shaw has been, for some time past, discussed with the interest which his work never fails to arouse. Mr. Shaw has his own views about the printing of work intended for the stage : he holds that the mere printing of the "prompt copy" is insufficient, and that "the institution of a new art" is necessary. So, in the two volumes now in the press, the customary meagre stage directions and scenic specifications will be found replaced by finished descriptions, vivid character-sketches, physiologic notes, sallies, and comments, in which the author's literary force is as conspicuous as in the dialogue. There is a lengthy introduction to the first volume, and prefaces to each play.

In Two Volumes.   Fcap. 8vo.   Cloth.   5s. each.

[Ready April 6.

∽ ∽

By VICTOR HUGO

Hernani

Translated into English Verse, with an Introduction
By R. Farquharson Sharp.

Small 4to.   Boards.   3s. 6d. net.   *[Ready.*

∽ ∽

By LOUISA SHORE

Hannibal

With Portrait in photogravure of the Author.

Mr. Frederic Harrison writes : "I have read and re-read 'Hannibal' with admiration. As a historical romance, carefully studied from the original histories, it is a noble conception of a great hero. . . . The merit of this piece is to have seized the historical conditions with such reality and such truth, and to have kept so sustained a flight at a high level of heroic dignity."

Crown 8vo.   Cloth.   5s. net.   *[Ready.*

8

Poetry

By LAURENCE BINYON

Author of "London Visions"

Porphyrion and other Poems

Crown 8vo.   Cloth.   5s. net.   [*Ready.*

∽ ∾

By WALTER LEAF, LL.D.

Versions from Hafiz

An Essay in Persian Metre

" For Hafiz, at least as much as for any poet," says Dr. Leaf in his introduction, "form is of the essence of his poetry," and an attempt is here made "to give English readers some idea of the most intimate and indissoluble bond of spirit and form " in his odes.   "And with it all one must try to convey some joint reminder of the fact that Hafiz is, as few poets have been, a master of words and rhythms."

Small 4to. Linen. 5s. net. *Also ten copies on Japanese vellum, numbered and signed by the Author,* 21s. net. [*Ready.*

∽ ∾

By EUGENE LEE-HAMILTON

Author of "Sonnets of the Wingless Hours," etc.

The Inferno of Dante translated with Plain Notes

Mr. Lee-Hamilton's aim has been to secure *a line-for-line translation.*
Fcap. 8vo.   Half Parchment.   5s. net.   [*Ready.*

∽ ∾

By LAURENCE HOUSMAN

Author of "Gods and their Makers," etc.

Spikenard

A Book of Devotional Love Poems

With Cover designed by the Author.
Small 4to.   Boards.   3s. 6d. net.   [*Ready.*

∽ ∾

By W. P. REEVES

Agent-General for New Zealand

New Zealand, and other Poems

Fcap. 8vo.   Paper Wrapper.   2s. net.   [*Ready.*

9

Poetry

BY KATHARINE TYNAN (MRS. HINKSON)

The Wind in the Trees
A Book of Country Verse

Fcap. 8vo.　Cloth.　3s. 6d. net.

❧　❧　❧

English Portraits

A SERIES OF LITHOGRAPHED DRAWINGS

BY

WILL ROTHENSTEIN

With an Introduction by the Artist, and Short Texts
by various hands.

❧　❧

The following Portraits are included in this Collection,
each from sittings specially given to Mr. Rothenstein :—

Mr. Grant Allen	Sir Henry Irving
Mr. William Archer	Mr. Henry James
Lord Charles Beresford, M.P.	Mr. W. E. H. Lecky, M.P.
Mr. Robert Bridges	Professor A. Legros
Mr. Walter Crane	Mrs. Meynell
Right Rev. Dr. Creighton	Mr. A. W. Pinero
Mr. Sidney Colvin	Sir Frederick Pollock
Mr. George Gissing	Mr. Charles Ricketts
Marchioness of Granby	Mr. John Sargent, R.A.
Sir F. Seymour Haden	Mr. Charles Haselwood Shannon
Mr. Thomas Hardy	Mr. George Bernard Shaw
Mr. W. E. Henley	Miss Ellen Terry

"Admirably life-like, . . . and the style of publication makes it very attractive."
—*Speaker.*

"The drawings are lithographs, rough sketches rather than elaborate drawings, but
they show that Mr. Rothenstein has thoroughly mastered his method, and knows how
to use it with most commendable self-restraint. They are admirable examples of the
style of drawing which he has made his own, and which has much to recommend it."
—*Scotsman.*

Folio.　In Buckram Cover specially designed by
the Artist.　35s. net.

Also in Parts, each containing Two Portraits.

2s. 6d. net.　　　　*[Ready.*

History

By The Rev. A. G. B. ATKINSON, M.A.

St. Botolph, Aldgate

*The Story of a City Parish, compiled from the Record
Books and other Ancient Documents. With a
Supplementary Chapter by the Vicar*

Crown 8vo. Cloth. 5s. net. [*Ready.*

∽ ∽ ∽

By TEMPLE SCOTT

A Bibliography of Omar Khayyam

With Prefatory Note by EDWARD CLODD, Ex-President of
the Omar Khayyam Club.

Fcap. 8vo. Buckram. 5s. net.

∽ ∽

EDITED BY W. T. STEAD

Letters from Julia

*Or, Light from the Borderland: a Series of Messages
as to the Life beyond the Grave received by
Automatic Writing from one
who has gone before*

16mo. Cloth. 2s.
[*Second Edition ready.*

11

ALLEN, GRANT.

Linnet: a Romance.   Crown 8vo.   Cloth.   6s.

The Evolution of the Idea of God: an Inquiry into the Origins of Religions.   Demy 8vo.   Buckram.   20s. net.   [*Second Edition.*

Grant Allen's Historical Guides:

Paris.	[*Ready.*
Florence.	,,
Cities of Belgium.	,,
Venice.	[*In preparation.*
Rome.	,,
Cities of Northern Italy.	,,

Fcap. 8vo.   Cloth.   3s. 6d. each, net.

"Good work in the way of showing students the right manner of approaching the history of a great city. . . . These useful little volumes."—*Times.*

"Those who travel for the sake of culture will be well catered for in Mr. Grant Allen's new series of historical guides. . . . There are few more satisfactory books for a student who wishes to dig out the Paris of the past from the immense superincumbent mass of coffee-houses, kiosks, fashionable hotels, and other temples of civilisation, beneath which it is now submerged.   Florence is more easily dug up, as you have only to go into the picture galleries, or into the churches or museums, whither Mr. Allen's guide accordingly conducts you, and tells you what to look at if you want to understand the art treasures of the city.   The books, in a word, explain rather than describe.   Such books are wanted nowadays. . . . The more sober-minded among tourists will be grateful to him for the skill with which the new series promises to minister to their needs."—*Scotsman.*

"Mr. Grant Allen, as a traveller of thirty-five years' experience in foreign lands, is well qualified to command success in the task he has set himself, and nothing in the two volumes under notice is more striking than the strong sense conveyed of his powers of observation and the facility with which he describes the objects of art and the architectural glories which he has met and lingered over. . . . It would be a pity indeed were his assiduous researches and the fruits of his immense experience, now so happily exemplified, to pass unnoticed either by 'globe trotters' or by students of art and history who have perforce to stay at home."—*Daily Telegraph.*

"No traveller going to Florence with any idea of understanding its art treasures, can afford to dispense with Mr. Grant Allen's guide.   He is so saturated with information gained by close observation and close study.   He is so candid, so sincere, so fearless, so interesting, and his little book is so portable and so pretty."—*Queen.*

"Not only admirable, but also, to the intelligent tourist, indispensable. . . . Mr. Allen has the artistic temperament. . . . With his origins, his traditions, his art criticisms, he goes to the heart of the matter, is outspoken concerning those things he despises, and earnest when describing those in which his soul delights. . . . *The books are genuinely interesting to the ordinary reader, whether he have travelled or not, and unlike the ordinary guide-book may be read with advantage both before and after the immediate occasion of their use.*"—*Birmingham Gazette*

13

Grant Richards's Publications

An African Millionaire: Episodes in the Life of the Illustrious Colonel Clay. With over Sixty Illustrations by Gordon Browne. Crown 8vo. Cloth. 6s. *[Fifth Edition.*

"It is not often that the short story of this class can be made as attractive and as exciting as are many of the Colonel's episodes. Let us be thankful for these, and hasten to commend ' An African Millionaire' to the notice of all travellers. We can imagine no book of the season more suitable for an afternoon in a hammock or a lazy day in the woods. And the capital illustrations help an excellent dozen of stories on their way."—*Daily Chronicle.*

"For resourcefulness, for sardonic humour, for a sense of the comedy of the situation, and for pluck to carry it through, it would be difficult to find a more entertaining scoundrel than Colonel Clay."—*Daily News.*

"This book is a good example of Mr. Grant Allen's talents. It is only a collection of tales describing how a very rich man is again and again victimised by the same adventurer, but it has not only plenty of dramatic incident, but of shrewd and wise reflection, such as is seldom found in the modern novel."—Mr. JAMES PAYN in the *Illustrated London News.*

ALMA TADEMA, LAURENCE.

Realms of Unknown Kings: Poems. Fcap. 8vo. Paper Wrapper. 2s. net. Buckram. 3s. net.

ANSTEY, F.

Paleface and Redskin, and other Stories for Boys and Girls. With Illustrations by Gordon Browne. *[In preparation.*

ATKINSON, A. G. B., M.A.

St. Botolph, Aldgate: The Story of a City Parish, compiled from the Record Books and other Ancient Documents. With a Supplementary Chapter by the Vicar. Crown 8vo. Cloth. 5s. net.

BELL, R. S. WARREN.

(*See* Henrietta Volumes.)

BINYON, LAURENCE.

Porphyrion and other Poems. Crown 8vo. Cloth. 5s. net.

BRETON, FREDERIC.

True Heart: a Novel. Crown 8vo. Cloth. 6s.

14

BROOK, EMMA.

A Tabulation of the Factory Laws of European Countries, in so far as they relate to the Hours of Labour and Special Legislation for Women, Young Persons, and Children. Demy 8vo. Half Cloth. 2s. 6d. net.

BURGIN, G. B.

The Cattle Man : a Novel.
"Old Man's" Marriage : A Novel. (A Sequel to "The Judge of the Four Corners.")
Crown 8vo. Cloth. 6s. each.

"Mr. Burgin's best qualities come to the front in '"Old Man's" Marriage.' . . . Miss Wilkes has nearly as much individuality as any one in the story, which is saying a good deal, for reality seems to gather round all the characters in spite of the romance that belongs to them as well . . . the story is fresh and full of charm."—*Standard.*

"Mr. Burgin's humour is both shrewd and kindly, and his book should prove as welcome as a breath of fresh air to the weary readers of realistic fiction."—*Daily Telegraph.*

"'Old Man's' Marriage is told with such humour, high spirit, simplicity, and straightforwardness that the reader is amused and entertained from the first page to the last. Once I had begun it I had to go on to the end; when I put it down it was with a sigh to part with such excellent company. . . . As thoroughly enjoyable and racily written a story as has been published for a long time."—Mr. COULSON KERNAHAN in the *Star.*

"It would be difficult to speak too highly of the delicate pathos and humour of this beautiful sketch of a choice friendship in humble life. . . . A study at once simple and subtle and full of the dignity and sincerity of natural man."—*Manchester Guardian.*

CLIFFORD, HUGH (British Resident at Pahang).

Studies in Brown Humanity : Being Scrawls and Smudges in Sepia, White, and Yellow. Crown 8vo. Cloth. 6s.

In Court and Kampong : Being Tales and Sketches of Native Life in the Malay Peninsula. Large Crown 8vo. Cloth. 7s. 6d.

"Mr. Clifford undoubtedly possesses the gift of graphic description in a high degree, and each one of these stories grips the reader's attention most insistently. The whole book is alive with drama and passion; but, as we have said, its greatest charm lies in the fact that it paints in strikingly minute detail a state of things which, whether for good or ill, is rapidly vanishing from the face of the earth."—*Speaker.*

"These tales Mr. Clifford tells with a force and life-likeness such as is only to be equalled in the stories of Rudyard Kipling. Take, for instance, the gruesome story of the were-tiger, man by day and man-eater by night. . . . Every one of these tales leaves its impression, dramatic yet lifelike. Moreover, they are valuable as giving a picture of strange, distorted civilisation which, under the influence of British residents and officials, will soon pass away or hide itself jealously from the gaze of Western eyes."—*Pall Mall Gazette.*

CLODD, EDWARD.

Pioneers of Evolution from Thales to Huxley,
with an intermediate chapter on the Causes of Arrest of the Movement. With portraits in photogravure of Charles Darwin, Professor Huxley, Mr. A. R. Wallace, and Mr. Herbert Spencer. Crown 8vo. Linen. 5s. net. *[Second Edition.*

"We are always glad to meet Mr. Edward Clodd. He is never dull; he is always well informed, and he says what he has to say with clearness and incision. . . . The interest intensifies as Mr. Clodd attempts to show the part really played in the growth of the doctrine of evolution by men like Wallace, Darwin, Huxley, and Spencer. Mr. Clodd clears away prevalent misconceptions as to the work of these modern pioneers. Especially does he give to Mr. Spencer the credit which is his due, but which is often mistakenly awarded to Darwin. Mr. Clodd does not seek in the least to lower Darwin from the lofty pedestal which he rightly occupies; he only seeks to show precisely why he deserves to occupy such a position. We commend the book to those who want to know what evolution really means; but they should be warned beforehand that they have to tackle strong meat."—*Times.*

"There is no better book on the subject for a general reader, and while its matter is largely familiar to professed students of science, and indeed to most men who are well read, no one could go through the book without being both refreshed and newly instructed by its masterly survey of the growth of the most powerful idea of modern times."—*Scotsman.*

CONSTABLE, F. C.

Aunt Judith's Island: a Comedy of Kith and Kin. Crown 8vo. Cloth. 6s.

DANTE.
(*See* Lee-Hamilton.)

DIXON, H. SYDENHAM ("Vigilant" of the *Sportsman*).

From Gladiateur to Persimmon: Turf History for Thirty Years. With portraits. Demy 8vo.

DUMPY BOOKS FOR CHILDREN.
Edited by E. V. Lucas, and with End-papers designed by Mrs. Farmiloe. 18mo. Cloth. 1s. 6d. each.

1. **The Flamp, the Ameliorator, and the Schoolboy's Apprentice: Three Stories.** By Edward Verrall Lucas.
2. **Mrs. Turner's Cautionary Stories.**

EGERTON, GEORGE.

The Wheel of God: a Novel. Crown 8vo. Cloth. 6s.

16

ETHICS OF THE SURFACE SERIES.

1. **The Rudeness of the Honourable Mr. Leatherhead.**
2. **A Homburg Story.**
3. **Cui Bono?**

By Gordon Seymour. 16mo. Buckram. 2s. each.

"The stories are remarkable for their originality, their careful characterisation, their genuine thoughtfulness, and the sincerity of their purpose. They certainly open up a fresh field of thought on the problems set by the philosopher of the superficial, problems which, though they seem to lie on the surface, strike their roots deep down into human life; and they make us think for ourselves (though perhaps somewhat gropingly), which is more than can be said for the general run of modern novels."—*Pall Mall Gazette.*

"An able and well-written little bit of fiction. . . . Amongst the short descriptive portions of the book there are some excellent examples of graceful prose, and if the dialogues occasionally resolve themselves into disquisitions on life and society too elaborate for the reader who is chiefly concerned to get the story, they will repay the reader who can appreciate the analysis of delicate shades of thought and feeling."—*Aberdeen Free Press.*

FLEMING, GEORGE.

Little Stories about Women. Crown 8vo. Cloth. 3s. 6d.

"All novel readers must welcome the decision which has caused these stories, many of which are gems, to appear in volume form. . . . Story is hardly the name to employ in the case of these impressionist pictures. They have the suggestive merit of the school and none of its vagueness."—*Morning Post.*

"It is impossible to read 'Little Stories about Women' without a feeling of blank astonishment that their author should be so very little more than a name to the reading public. . . . It is difficult to imagine anything better in its way—and its way is thoroughly modern and up to date—than the first of the collection, 'By Accident.' It is very short, very terse, but the whole story is suggested with admirable art. There is nothing unfinished about it, and the grip with which the carriage accident which opens it is presented never relaxes."—*World.*

GILCHRIST, R. MURRAY.   (*See* Sylvan Series.)

HENRIETTA VOLUMES, THE.

The Cub in Love: in Twelve Twinges; with Six additional Stories. By R. S. Warren Bell. With Cover by Maurice Greiffenhagen. Tauchnitz size. 1s. 6d. (*Copies also obtainable in Cloth.* 2s.)

"Light and amusing withal is Mr. Warren Bell's sketch of a very young man suffering from the bitter-sweet of an unrequited affection. . . . The Cub seems to be a near relation of Dolly (of the 'Dolly Dialogues'), and the sprightliness of his dialogue makes him worthy of the kinship."—*Pall Mall Gazette.*

"The book makes excellent reading for travelling or a holiday, or, indeed, for any occasion on which amusement is the thing desired. If the subsequent volumes of the Henrietta series are up to this standard, there need be no question of their success."—*Scotsman.*

"This is one of the most brightly written books we have read for some time. . . . We cannot conceive a more enjoyable book for a couple of hours' reading at the seaside."—*Belfast Evening Telegraph.*

HOUSMAN, LAURENCE.

Spikenard: a Book of Devotional Love Poems. With Cover designed by the Author. Small 4to. Boards. 3s. 6d. net.

H.R.H. The Prince of Wales: an Account of His Career, including his Birth, Education, Travels, Marriage, and Home Life and Philanthropic, Social, and Political Work. Royal 8vo. Cloth. 10s. 6d. With one hundred Portraits and other Illustrations.

HUGO, VICTOR.

Hernani: a Drama, translated into English Verse, with an Introduction by R. Farquharson Sharp. Small 4to. Boards. 3s. 6d. net.

LEAF, WALTER, LL.D.

Versions from Hafiz: an Essay in Persian Metre. Small 4to. Linen. 5s. net. (*Also Ten Copies on Japanese Vellum, numbered and signed by the Author, 21s. net.*)

LEAKE, MRS. PERCY.

The Ethics of Browning's Poems. With Introduction by the Bishop of Winchester. Fcap. 8vo. Cloth. 2s. 6d.

LEE, VERNON.

Limbo and other Essays. With Frontispiece. Fcap. 8vo. Buckram. 5s. net.

"The brilliant and versatile writer who adopts the pseudonym of Vernon Lee affords a dainty feast to her readers in this charming little volume."—*Times.*

"For charm, that 'delicate and capricious foster-child of leisure,' Vernon Lee's latest work, small as it is, is the equal of anything that she has yet produced."—*Morning Post.*

"This little volume might be called a manual of the cultivated soul adventuring among masterpieces of art and natural beauties. It brings to the enjoyment of these a power of association which traverses seas and years, and refreshes the mind with images summoned from the recesses of memory. They are pitched in a pleasant conversational way, frankly, even daringly, personal, and are strewn with vivid descriptions of Italian scenes and places."—*Manchester Guardian.*

"'Limbo and other Essays' is amongst the most welcome of recent books. . . . Few essayists see so many beautiful things as Vernon Lee, and fewer still, having seen them, say so many beautiful things about them."—Mr. RICHARD LE GALLIENNE in the *Star.*

LEE-HAMILTON, EUGENE.

The Inferno of Dante translated with Plain Notes. Fcap. 8vo. Half Parchment. 5s. net.

Grant Richards's Publications

LE GALLIENNE, RICHARD.

Rubaiyat of Omar Khayyam : a Paraphrase from several Literal Translations. From the press of Messrs. T. and A. Constable of Edinburgh. Long Fcap. 8vo. Parchment. 5s. Also a very limited Edition on Japanese Vellum, numbered and signed by the Author. 15s. net. [*All sold.*

LEIGHTON, MARIE CONNOR and ROBERT.

Convict 99 : a Novel. With Eight full-page Illustrations by Stanley L. Wood. Crown 8vo. Cloth. 3s. 6d.

LOWNDES, FREDERIC SAWREY.

Bishops of the Day : a Biographical Dictionary of the Archbishops and Bishops of the Church of England, and of all Churches in Communion therewith throughout the World. Fcap. 8vo. Cloth. 5s.

"While the assembly of nearly 200 Bishops of the Anglican Communion at the Lambeth Conference makes the publication of the volume at the present time especially opportune, Mr. Lowndes's work is likely to command a more permanent interest. It gives a full and lucid sketch of the career of each Bishop, without any suggestion of partisan bias on the part of the author."—*Times.*

"Few works of reference could be more acceptable to Churchmen of the present time. . . . Plenty of dates of the right sort, as well as matters of more human interest."—*Guardian.*

"The work is thoroughly up to date, as one may see from the Episcopal events of 1896 and 1897 here recorded. It abounds in personal incidents and anecdotes not to be found elsewhere, and evidently derived from original and accredited sources. . . . Much valuable information on Church matters generally incidental to Episcopal administration."—*Morning Post.*

"Mr. Lowndes has spared no pains to make his compendium as perfect as possible. . . . This book is, as far as we can know, the first of the kind that has been published, and supplies, in good time, a want that would have soon become urgent."—*Standard.*

"Valuable for reference on account of much of the information contained in the neatly got-up volume being supplied by the prelates themselves."—*World.*

"The book should be bought and read at once. There is no Churchman whom it will not interest, and it contains a sufficiency of blank spaces to admit of MS. additions, which may record the inevitable changes brought about by death or by translation. Mr. Lowndes deserves our very cordial thanks for a piece of work which few would have undertaken, and none could have achieved more perfectly."—*Sheffield Daily Telegraph.*

LUCAS, EDWARD VERRALL.

A Book of Verses for Children. With Cover, Title-page, and End-papers designed in colours by F. D. Bedford. Crown 8vo. Cloth. 6s.
[*Third Edition.*

(*See also* Dumpy Books for Children.)

MACFALL, HALDANE.

The Wooings of Jezebel Pettyfer: a Novel. Crown 8vo. Cloth. 6s.

MAETERLINCK, MAURICE.

Aglavaine and Selysette: a Drama in Five Acts. Translated by Alfred Sutro. With Introduction by J. W. Mackail, and Title-page designed by W. H. Margetson. Globe 8vo. Half Buckram. 2s. 6d. net.

"To read the play is to have one's sense of beauty quickened and enlarged, to he touched hy the inward and spiritual grace of things. . . . Mr. Sutro is the most conscientious, and at the same time the most ambitious, of translators; not content with reproducing the author's thought, he strives after the same effect of language—the plaintive note, the dying cadence, the Maeterlincked sweetness long drawn out. And more often than not he succeeds,—which is saying a good deal when one considers the enormous difficulties of the task."—Mr. A. B. WALKLEY in the *Speaker*.

"The book is a treasury of beautiful things. No one now writing loves beauty as M. Maeterlinck does. Sheer, essential beauty has no such lover. He will have nothing else."—*Academy*.

"Mr. Alfred Sutro's careful and delicate translation of M. Maurice Maeterlinck's new play gives readers of English every opportunity of appreciating a work which, so to speak, is at the tip of the century. . . . The book, as a whole, is perhaps the best yet published by which an English-speaking stranger to M. Maeterlinck could make his acquaintance."—*Scotsman*.

MERRICK, LEONARD.

The Actor-Manager: a Novel. Crown 8vo. Cloth. 6s.

One Man's View: a Novel. Cr. 8vo. Cloth. 3s. 6d.

"A novel over which we could at a pinch fancy ourselves sitting up till the small hours. . . . The characters are realised, the emotion is felt and communicated."—*Daily Chronicle*.

"An uncommonly well-written story. . . . The men in the book are excellent, and the hero . . . is an admirable portrait."—*Standard*.

"Mr. Leonard Merrick's work is exceptionally good: his style is literary, he has insight into character, and he can touch on delicate matters without being coarse or unpleasantly suggestive. 'One Man's View' is keenly interesting. . . . 'One Man's View' is one of those rare books in which, without a superfluous touch, each character stands out clear and individually. It holds the reader's attention from first to last."—*Guardian*.

MEYNELL, ALICE.

The Flower of the Mind: a Choice among the best Poems. With Cover designed by Laurence Housman. Crown 8vo. Buckram. 6s.

"Partial collections of English poems, decided by a common subject or bounded by the dates and periods of literary history, are made more than once in every year, and the makers are safe from the reproach of proposing their own personal taste as a guide for the reading of others. But a general Anthology gathered from the whole of English literature—the whole from Chaucer to Wordsworth—by a gatherer intent upon nothing except the quality of poetry, is a more rare attempt."—*Extract from Introduction*.

MORROW, W. C.
>   **The Ape, the Idiot, and other People.** Crown
>   8vo. Cloth. 6s.

OMAN, DR. J. CAMPBELL.
>   **Where Three Creeds Meet:** a Tale of Indian
>   Life. Crown 8vo. Cloth. 3s. 6d.

READ, CARVETH, M.A.
>   **Logic: Deductive and Inductive.** Crown 8vo.
>   Cloth. 6s.

REEVES, W. P.
>   **New Zealand, and other Poems.** Fcap. 8vo.
>   Paper Wrapper. 2s. net.

ROTHENSTEIN, WILL.
>   **English Portraits:** a Series of Lithographed
>   Drawings. With an Introduction by the Artist, and
>   Short Texts by various hands. Folio. In Buckram
>   Cover designed by the Artist. 35s. net. Or in
>   Twelve Parts, 2s. 6d. each, net. (*See p.* 10.)

"The portraits, which are of a large portfolio size, are vivid likenesses, and their appearance is a gratifying indication of the revival of lithography in fine art."—*Aberdeen Free Press.*

"The introductory examples fulfil to the full the promises made in the publisher's announcements, and it is certain that the series will be keenly appreciated by art lovers."—*Dundee Advertiser.*

SCOTT, TEMPLE.
>   **A Bibliography of Omar Khayyam.** With a
>   Prefatory Note by Edward Clodd. Fcap. 8vo.
>   Buckram. 5s. net.

SCHWARTZE, HELMUTH.
>   **The Laughter of Jove:** a Novel. Cr. 8vo. Cl. 6s.

SEYMOUR, GORDON.
>   (*See* Ethics of the Surface Series.)

SHAW, GEORGE BERNARD.
>   **Plays: Pleasant and Unpleasant.**
>   >   I. Unpleasant.   II. Pleasant.
>   With special Introduction, Prefaces to each Play, and
>   a portrait of the Author in photogravure. Fcap.
>   8vo. Cloth. 5s. each.
>   (*See also* Politics in 1896.)

SHIEL, M. P.

The Yellow Danger: a Novel. Crown 8vo. Cloth. 6s.

SHORE, ARABELLA and LOUISA.

Poems by A. and L. Crown 8vo. Cloth. 5s. net.

SHORE, LOUISA.

Hannibal: a Poetical Drama in Two Parts. New Edition. With Portrait. Crown 8vo. Cloth. 5s. net.

SPENCER, EDWARD ("Nathaniel Gubbins").

Cakes and Ale: a Memory of Many Meals; the whole interspersed with various recipes, more or less original, and anecdotes, many veracious. With Cover designed by Phil May. Small 4to. Cloth. 5s.
[Third Edition.

"Exceedingly readable, clever, and, moreover, highly informative. . . . From racy chapter to racy chapter the reader is irresistibly carried on. . . . The mistress of the house will read it carefully for the sake of the valuable recipes and hints, and mine host will esteem it for the smart style in which it is written, and for the plenitude of humour displayed in anecdote, story, and reminiscence."—*Dundee Advertiser.*

"Allow me to say that it is a little book on a great subject that deserves to occupy an honourable place in every library, on the same shelf as Kettner's 'Book of the Table,' Sala's 'A Thorough Good Cook,' and perhaps that over-praised but un-doubtedly entertaining classic, 'Gastronomy as a Fine Art,' by Brillat-Savarin."—*Sporting Life.*

"This little volume should have its place among the wedding presents of every bride."—*Lady's Pictorial.*

"There are many useful hints on table matters, and the recipes are all eminently practical. No country house should be without it."—*Guardian.*

STEAD, W. T.

Real Ghost Stories: a Revised Reprint of the Christmas and New Year Numbers of the "Review of Reviews," 1891-92. With new Intro-duction. Crown 8vo. Cloth. 5s.

Letters from Julia ; or, Light from the Border-land: a Series of Messages as to Life beyond the Grave received by Automatic Writing from one who has gone before. 16mo. Cloth. 2s. *[Second Edition.*

Grant Richards's Publications

STILLMAN, W. J.

The Old Rome and the New, and other Studies. Crown 8vo. Cloth. 5s.

SYLVAN SERIES, THE.

A Peakland Faggot: Tales told of Milton Folk. By R. Murray Gilchrist. Fcap. 8vo. Cloth. 2s. 6d.

"Not only are the sketches themselves full of charm and real literary value, but the little volume is as pleasant to the eye and to the touch as its contents are stimulating to the imagination. . . . We do not envy the person who could lay down the book without feeling refreshed in spirit by its perusal. . . . We cannot give our readers better counsel than in advising them to procure without delay this charming and cheery volume."—*Speaker.*

"We have no hesitation in saying that this is the very best work which Mr. Gilchrist has given us. As studies of Black Country character it is superb. In fact he is a master of our feelings and emotions in this daintily produced little volume, and 'A Peakland Faggot' will solidify that reputation which he has been steadily building up of late years. The style is thoroughly poetic. . . . Our hearty congratulations to Mr. Murray Gilchrist upon this performance—the magic he has used is the magic of true genius."—*Birmingham Gazette.*

"The writer who gives us glimpses into the psychology of the poor and illiterate ought always to be welcome. . . . Mr. Murray Gilchrist has introduced us to a new world of profound human interest."—Mr. T. P. O'CONNOR in the *Graphic.*

"I have read no book outside Mr. Hardy's so learned in such minutiæ of country 'wit' and sentiment."—Mr. RICHARD LE GALLIENNE in the *Star.*

TROUBRIDGE, LADY.

Paul's Stepmother, and One Other Story. With Frontispiece by Mrs. Adrian Hope. Crown 8vo. Cloth. 3s. 6d.

"There is a fine natural interest in both these stories, and Lady Troubridge recounts them so well and gracefully that to the critical reader this interest is greatly enhanced."—*Dundee Advertiser.*

"It is with a genuine feeling of pleasure that the reader will linger over 'Paul's Stepmother,' a story that one is inclined to wish were longer. . . . The pathos of the situation is treated with real feeling, and there is not a discordant note throughout the story. . . . Both stories are marked as the work of a fine and cultured writer."—*Weekly Sun.*

TURNER, ELIZABETH.

(*See* Dumpy Books for Children.)

WALDSTEIN, LOUIS, M.D.

The Subconscious Self and its Relation to Education and Health. Fcap. 8vo. Cloth. 3s. 6d.

WARBOROUGH, MARTIN LEACH.

Tom, Unlimited: a Story for Children. With Fifty Illustrations by Gertrude Bradley. Globe 8vo. Cloth. 5s.

23

WEBB, SIDNEY.

Labour in the Longest Reign (1837 - 1897).
Issued under the Auspices of the Fabian Society.
Fcap. 8vo. Cloth. 1s.

"It is, considering the source from which it comes, a singularly temperate and just review of the changes in the lot of the labourer which the reign has brought."—*Scotsman.*

"Mr. Sidney Webb has set forth some expert and telling comparisons between the condition of the working-classes in 1837 and 1897. His remarks on wages, on the irregularity of employment, on hours of labour, and on the housing of the poor, are worthy of earnest consideration."—*Daily Mail.*

WHELEN, FREDERICK (Editor).

Politics in 1896. With Contributions by H. D. Traill, D.C.L.; H. W. Massingham; G. Bernard Shaw; G. W. Steevens; H. W. Wilson; Captain F. N. Maude; Albert Shaw, and Robert Donald. Globe 8vo. Cloth. 3s. net.

"For more reasons than one Mr. Whelen's Political Annual, of which the present is the first issue, deserves a welcome. Not only does it constitute a handy work of reference, that besides merely enumerating the political wants of the past year shows also the light in which they are regarded by various shades of public opinion, but it calls for recognition as a record of the development of political thought, that, if regularly issued, will be of value to the future historian. . . . The book has attractions for those who wish to understand the various ideas actuating contending parties, and such readers will certainly find entertaining matter in the several contributions."—*Morning Post.*

"Mr. Whelen has undertaken a difficult task, but the volume which he has just issued is a very interesting and useful retrospect, and all who are interested in contemporary affairs will be glad to know that it is intended to be an annual. The plan is simple and comprehensive. . . . Mr. Whelen has done a useful work in starting this adventure, and we wish him all success."—*Daily Chronicle.*

"Those who can afford it, which includes at least every Labour Club, ought to possess a copy for their library."—Mr. KEIR HARDIE in the *Labour Leader.*

WHITTEN, WILFRED.

London in Song: an Anthology of Prose and Poetry inspired by London. With an Introduction. Crown 8vo. Buckram. 6s. [*In Preparation.*

WILLSON, BECKLES.

The Tenth Island: Being some Account of Newfoundland; its People, its Politics, and its Peculiarities. With an Introduction by Sir William Whiteway, K.C.M.G., Premier of the Colony, and an Appendix by Lord Charles Beresford. Globe 8vo. Buckram. 3s. 6d. With Map.

Printed by R. & R. CLARK, LIMITED, *Edinburgh.*